WILD
HORSES
OF Half-Moon RANCH

CHIQUITITA

CHIQUITITA

Jenny Oldfield

Illustrated by Paul Hunt

Hodder
Children's
Books

a division of Hodder Headline Limited

Copyright © 2001 Jenny Oldfield
Illustrations copyright © 2001 Paul Hunt

First published in Great Britain in 2001
by Hodder Children's Books

10 9 8 7 6 5 4 3 2 1

A Catalogue record for this book is available from the British Library

ISBN 0 340 79597 2

Typeset by Avon Dataset Ltd, Bidford-on-Avon, Warks

Printed and bound in Great Britain by
The Guernsey Press Co. Ltd, Channel Isles

Hodder Children's Books
a division of Hodder Headline Limited
338 Euston Road
London NW1 3BH

1

'This one is especially for Rob,' Wayne Raburn said. He was leading a small group of three riders along the shore of Squaw Lake. The sun was rising in a delicate pink sky – no mist and not a cloud in sight. 'I want this horse to be a big surprise for my boy when he gets back from the city.'

Kirstie Scott and Lisa Goodman followed quietly, drowsily in tune with the gentle trot of their horses. Early morning wasn't Lisa's best time. In fact, when Kirstie glanced at her friend, she thought maybe she'd fallen asleep in the saddle. She reached out and poked her in the ribs, making her squeak and sit up.

'Huh! What happened? What did I do?' Lisa hissed.

'Almost fell off your horse and broke your neck, is all!' Kirstie grinned. Then she trotted ahead to join Wayne.

'How come Rob gets to have a mustang all to himself?' she asked.

Wayne smiled. 'Why, are you jealous?'

'No – well, OK then, yeah!' Kirstie's red-faced admission made Wayne chuckle. 'Who wouldn't be?' she stammered. 'I mean, to be the owner of a genuine wild horse, fresh off the Nevada desert – well, wow!'

'Yeah, as you say, wow!' The girls' host during their summer vacation stay at Squaw Lake changed direction and headed his horse towards a western ridge. 'This mustang will be to die for, huh?'

'So is Rob's birthday coming up?' Kirstie persisted with her original question. 'Is that why he had to visit his grandfather?'

She, Lisa and Wayne had returned from Sunset Creek, a ranch near Tamapo, to discover that Wayne's son, Rob, had taken off to California with his grandmother. It had been a surprise decision, and one which seemed to worry Wayne.

'No. His birthday's in May,' he told Kirstie. 'Accordin' to Walter and the note Rob left for me, Rob's grandma didn't drive all the way up from San Francisco on a purely social visit. She brought news that his grandpa was sick and wanted to see him.'

'Tough!' Kirstie murmured. You always knew that your grandparents were old, but somehow you were never ready for the time when they fell sick.

'It's his mom's dad,' Wayne explained. 'Rob spends a lot of time with his grandparents during term time when he lives with his mom in the city.'

Kirstie nodded. 'So this surprise will help to keep him from worrying. That's cool.'

'Glad you think so.' Wayne reined back his horse to wait for Lisa, who seemed to have dozed off again. 'Walter made it clear that I was spoilin' the boy.'

'No way!' Kirstie didn't have much time for Wayne's sour, surly assistant. He was the type of guy who didn't say much, but probably thought a lot of things, most of them critical.

'Hmm. I guess he figures it'll be one more mouth to feed. I told him it was no extra work for him, just for me and Rob. Anyhow, come next spring, Walter won't be here.'

Kirstie shrugged and dismissed the subject. 'Hey, Lisa!' she called. 'We gotta find ourselves the ideal mustang for Rob!'

'I heard what Wayne said.' Lisa trotted up, pretending that she'd been wide awake all along. 'It's Rob's birthday treat.'

'Yeah, whatever!' Kirstie giggled.

'So how do we do this exactly?' Lisa wanted to know. She waved her free arm around the whole basin area. 'Like, big desert – small horse!'

Squaw Lake was set in a scooped out dish of land just east of the Sierra Nevada. Many millions of years ago, giant icebergs had scraped into the rock, dumping strange heaps of debris and leaving weird pinnacles of harder granite pointing skywards. When the glaciers had eventually melted, they'd turned into vast freshwater lakes like the ones the girls were riding beside right now.

'C'mon, Lisa, don't give me that!' Wayne grumbled. 'Didn't I teach you anythin' in the weeks you bin here?'

'Yeah. You taught me to wear high-factor sunblock!' she cheeked him, knowing that he would take it. 'But I still got freckles, didn't I?'

' "Big desert – small horse!" ' Wayne mimicked in a helpless girly voice. Then he played along. 'Ooh look, here's a hoofprint! And over there by the thornbushes are more of those round, hoof shaped marks!'

'Doh!' Lisa hit her forehead with the heel of her hand. 'You mean, we track the herd!'

'Quit fooling around, you two!' Kirstie stopped to give her sorrel quarter-horse a break. She took off her straw hat and fanned her face. 'Seriously Wayne, we can find the wild herd, no problem. But how d'you select the one you want, cut him out and bring him back to Squaw Lake for Rob?'

'It ain't easy,' he admitted. 'I'm not sayin' it is. A mustang is a herd animal. He sticks with the rest and they don't miss a single thing that's goin' on around them. So even gettin' close is hard.'

'And when we do, what then?' Kirstie tried to foresee the day ahead. She figured they would pick up the herd by midday and then have the job of bringing one back home before nightfall. But she didn't have a clear idea of the details. 'We don't rope him, do we?'

Wayne shook his head. 'Between the three of

us, we cut him out from the herd and run with him until he's ready to parley.'

'Uh-oh, Snowbird, did you hear that?' Lisa said, patting her Appaloosa's neck. 'Wayne said we have to "run" with a mustang in the midday heat. Does that sound tough, or what?'

'Go back to sleep,' Kirstie kidded. She liked the idea of getting in amongst the magnificent wild herd, of having a close-up view of the wild horses' long, high tails, their rising and falling manes as they ran for the sheer pleasure of feeling the wind. 'When the horse is ready to talk, d'you work with him out here on the open range?'

'That's the plan,' Wayne grinned. 'Then, when he's ready, old Prince here helps me to drop a rope round his neck. We school the mustang to dally along nice and quiet and then we head for home.'

Kirstie took a look at Wayne's big, dark bay horse. Prince was kind of clunky and bony, and all of sixteen hands high. Dainty he was not.

'You think he can't do it?' Wayne challenged, picking up speed across a dry, open stretch of ground. By now they'd left the lake far behind and were making for a clear exit from the basin between two tall rocks. 'OK, so how about you and Fresno doin' the job?'

'No, thanks!' she answered hastily. 'That horse whispering part is down to you. You're the wild horse expert, and I don't want to be the one who loses us Rob's mustang!'

Wayne grinned back at them both. 'First, find your herd!' he called, setting off at a lope, raising dust.

'First, eat dirt!' Lisa grunted. She ducked to avoid the flying grit from Prince's hooves, then she and Kirstie fanned wide on Snowbird and Fresno, challenging Wayne to a flat out race.

'OK, so you never came out this way before, did you?' Once out of Squaw Lake Basin, Wayne had given the horses a breather. All three riders had dismounted and were gazing west towards the foothills of the Sierra Nevada now bathed in early morning sunlight. The space in between was filled with sagebrush and chaparral scrub, with a few juniper and pinon pine trees scattered here and there.

Lisa and Kirstie shook their heads. Turning directly to the south, Kirstie could make out a landmark called Thunder Rock and was able to judge how far from familiar territory their group had ridden. 'Has the herd been seen over this way?' she asked Wayne.

He nodded. 'A lady called Mary Ellen Black owns a spread named Hope Valley over in the foothills. She flew over in a light aircraft late last night, called me to say the mustangs were heading her way and could I head them off before they ate all that was left of her grass.'

'And you said OK.' Lisa understood that they would be doing the lady rancher a favour and keeping in with the local landowners, some of whom kicked up a fuss about the government controlled wild herd. Wayne headed up the Western Nevada Bureau of Land Management, and part of his job was to try and keep the ranchers happy. The rest of it was to protect the wild horses from would-be rustlers and to manage the size of the herd.

'Yep. Mary Ellen said she'd be mighty grateful. She also told me that she'd have men with guns out along her fence line, ready to eliminate any mustangs that stepped on to her land.'

'No, really!' Kirstie gasped.

'Yeah. Mary Ellen ain't a shrinkin' violet. In fact, she's tougher'n most guys who own land around here. I needed to remind her that shootin' a mustang was a criminal activity. "So," she says, "you head 'em off before they reach here tomorrow mornin', Wayne, and keep me outta gaol as long as you can!" '

Lisa glanced at Prince, Snowbird and Fresno quietly grazing nearby. 'Like, why don't we head out?' she asked nervously. 'The sound of coming up against men with guns waiting on the fence line doesn't grab me as a great way to end my vacation!'

Grinning, Wayne agreed on a remount. 'Did Rob ever tell you about the Water Cave?' he asked as they rode on.

Lisa and Kirstie shook their heads.

'We're comin' up to it over the next ridge. It's the big landmark hereabouts, and one reason why the horses head out this way.'

'Because there's water?' Kirstie guessed.

'And a cave!' Lisa added with a grin. 'Like, wow!'

'OK, so I won't tell you the story,' Wayne teased.

'Go ahead, I wanna hear it,' Kirstie insisted.

'It's the site of some cave dwellings, maybe

inhabited by the Zuni people way back. They came up from the south west and tunnelled into the rocks. It's like a honeycomb in there, with dozens of cave paintings and drawings carved into the rocks.'

'Do tourists come to look at the place?' Kirstie asked.

'Some, but not many. The only way out here is on horseback. Most people on vacation like to hire a Jeep and take it easy. Horseriding isn't on their list.'

Quickly Kirstie turned to Lisa. 'Don't say a word!' she warned.

Lisa looked as if her feelings had been hurt. 'Would I?'

'So the Water Cave is pretty deserted, and you get a real spooky feelin' when you ride by,' Wayne went on, with a mischievous look on his handsome, tanned face. 'You get to pick up all the spirits of the ancient people hauntin' the tunnels, floating' in the air and lookin' down on you. Like a thousand pairs of eyes belongin' to dead people, and the wind sounds like voices in among the caves.'

Lisa frowned and began to look around more cautiously.

'What about the Water Cave itself?' Kirstie asked. She adored the old Native American stories. Besides, she knew Lisa spooked easily.

'Yeah, the Water Cave . . .' Wayne hesitated, listened, then changed direction slightly. 'There's a big heap of rock blocking the entrance to this particular cave which overlooks a small lake, called Great Bird Lake, about a quarter of the size of Squaw Lake. The rocks are too big for any man to have moved there. So the Zuni story goes that an evil spirit dumped them at the entrance to keep other spirits out.'

'What kind of evil spirit?' Kirstie asked, checking to see that Lisa was listening.

'Now this one is a cannibal and a bone-crusher. Some say he takes the shape of a great bird, and so they named the lake after him. But another story goes that the spirit who lives in the cave is a water baby. She's a female, and in spite of her name, she's pure evil.'

'Why, what does she do?' Lisa wanted to know, her green eyes wide and staring. She rode Snowbird close up alongside Wayne.

He clicked his tongue against his teeth, taking his time to answer. 'Well, she's small, with long hair down to the ground. She lives by herself . . .'

'But what does she *do*?' Again, Lisa pressed for a reply.

'She creates the hot springs that you find around here.'

Lisa was confused. 'But that's not evil, is it?'

'. . . And, she comes along at night and steals the tribespeople's unguarded babies.'

'Oh, gruesome!' Lisa gasped.

'And she pulls people into the lake in broad daylight!' Wayne announced as they crested the ridge and looked down on a small expanse of water.

'Yugh!' Lisa shook herself. 'That's evil with a capital E!' she agreed.

'Yeah, and it gets worse. The water baby was hooked up with a giant water serpent who grabbed a hold of her victims and dragged them down into the deep, crushing their bones and spitting them up to the surface a piece at a time. Then his girlfriend took them and stored them in a giant heap inside her cave. That's why she piled the rocks high across the entrance, so nobody could rescue the bones of their loved ones . . .'

'Now you're making it up!' Lisa protested.

'I swear I'm not.' Wayne rode ahead towards the innocent-looking lake. Its clear water sparkled in the sun, and behind it a steep, stepped cliff rose to a height of about a hundred feet.

'At least the cave dwelling part is true,' Kirstie said, pointing out square entrances carved into the cliff. The whole thing was some eighty to a hundred yards long, and there were narrow shelves of rock carved into its face, with steps between levels and small square windows cut out to let the light into the primitive dwellings.

'Jeez, it looks like a kid tried to build a modern tower block out of clay!' Lisa took in the strange sight. 'But they got the levels a little wobbly and when they put it in the oven to bake, it all cracked and toppled sideways!'

'Here are the drawings you talked about.' Kirstie had ridden close to the foot of the cliff and now pointed out some pale marks scratched into the surface. There were human figures, a man on a horse, a deer and even a wheel, all simply drawn.

'Hey, and look at this one. It's a giant pair of eyes.' Lisa hadn't noticed that she had halted Snowbird beside a tall heap of boulders, which blocked the entrance to a huge cave. She was too

13

busy working out the shapes etched into the lowest boulder to realise where she was. 'Here are two eyes with circles around them, and a nose and a mouth . . .'

Wayne and Kirstie rode over to examine the drawing.

'Yeah, that's the water baby,' Wayne said calmly.

Lisa jumped a mile and propelled Snowbird backwards into the water that lay at the foot of the rocks.

Wayne grinned. 'Don't worry. They say a Zuni shaman worked up a spell that turned her into stone. Now she can watch everyone who passes by Great Bird Lake, but she can't do a darned thing to harm them.'

'Come out of the lake, Lisa!' Kirstie called sweetly.

Snowbird thrashed around in the cold water, trying to find his balance.

'I'm tryin'!' Lisa cried.

'Don't fall in. There's a water serpent behind you, ready to crush your bones!'

'Aagh!' There was a wild shriek as water splashed over Lisa's head and shoulders. 'Get me out of here!'

So Wayne and Kirstie rode into the lake like the US cavalry to the rescue. One on either side, they grabbed Snowbird's bridle, turned him around and walked him steadily out of the water.

'C'mon, let's cowboy up,' Wayne said to a dripping Lisa and a laughing Kirstie. He too was grinning from ear to ear. 'It's seven thirty and we still got us a wild horse to find!'

2

'Trust Wayne to pick out my dream horse!' Kirstie
sighed.

The moment she'd set eyes on the little black-
and-white paint amongst the herd, which was
quietly grazing on a plateau about three miles from
Great Bird Lake, she'd fallen in love with her.

First off, the mustang's markings cut her out
from the rest. Her head was mostly black, with a
pale muzzle. There were patches of black on her
neck, chest and hindquarters, but her front legs,
belly and back were pure white. Her mane and tail
were a streaked blend of both colours.

So she looked different from the run-of-the-mill sorrels and bays. But it was more than that. When Wayne had pointed her out and said, 'That's the one!' Kirstie had recognised a certain proud spirit in the way she held her head. She'd reared up as the three riders had approached the herd, and pranced a few steps towards them before she'd landed then disappeared into the melée.

'Why the paint?' Lisa had asked, trying to pick her out again. The whole herd was in a state of high alert, milling around restlessly and looking to their leaders for the signal to take flight.

'Because!' Wayne had answered. He'd pulled Lisa and Kirstie downwind of the herd to allow them to settle.

'She's stunning!' Kirstie said, still with a picture in her head of the little mare rearing and prancing. 'Rob will really love her.'

'OK, so you tell me!' Lisa whispered to Kirstie, while Wayne kept his eye on the movements of the herd. 'What's so special?'

'Good conformation,' Kirstie explained. 'Broad shoulders, strong, straight legs, powerful hindquarters. She's probably around four years old, and pretty too. That's a good combination.'

'Anything else I should know?' Lisa was serious in wanting to learn more. Her vacation had infected her with a love of the wild horses of Nevada almost as great as Kirstie's own.

'Just a feeling,' Kirstie shrugged. 'This isn't to do with technical stuff, it's more a gut reaction. I could tell you about the look in her eye, but it wouldn't make much sense. I just figure she's gonna be a fun horse.'

'Yeah, fun to catch too,' Wayne murmured as the herd bunched together and began to move east. Slowly at first, they left off grazing and the mares collected their foals, ready to leave. Then the leader of the herd, a white mare, headed them across the plateau, back in the direction Wayne and the girls had just come.

Amongst the two hundred or so horses, the chosen paint still stood out. She'd positioned herself at the far side of the herd, near to the front, and Wayne had to decide how to cut her out without causing a stampede.

'Maybe they're making for Great Bird Lake,' Lisa suggested. 'We could separate the paint out while they're drinking on the shore.'

Wayne nodded. 'Good thinkin'. And it saves

Mary Ellen's guys the trouble of havin' to shoot any of 'em.' He grinned wryly. 'C'mon. Let's ride south east and work up from a new direction, catch them off guard.'

So they reined Prince, Snowbird and Fresno towards a bare slope of grey scree and a rocky horizon, looping around the bottom end of the lake and riding up from the south. A hard gallop of fifteen minutes brought them to the shore before the herd was even in sight.

'Where do we hide?' Kirstie asked Wayne, scanning the open landscape.

'In amongst the cave dwellings would be good,' he decided, leading the way around the edge of the blue water, past the Water Cave, and up the slope towards the houses that had been tunnelled into the rock. Straggling aspen trees grew at the foot of the cliff, providing enough shelter for the three riders to hide themselves and wait patiently for the herd to arrive.

'I sure hope they're headed this way!' Lisa muttered, beginning to lose faith in her own theory.

But Kirstie worked out that her friend had been right from the way her horse's head was facing west, listening carefully to a sound that couldn't yet be picked up by the human ear.

'Here they come!' Wayne announced, pointing to a cloud of dust on the horizon. Then he pulled Prince further in under the cliff and waited.

Soon the wild horses came into full view, covering the ground at an easy lope, anticipating an unhurried cool drink before the sun gained strength. It would send them refreshed on their way to their next grazing spot, which could be any place on the thousands of square miles set aside by the Bureau of Land Management for the precious wild breed.

Kirstie held Fresno on a short rein as the thundering hooves drew near. Her sorrel gelding eased back under the cliff, well hidden by the trees.

Lisa too followed Wayne's lead. She soothed Snowbird with a series of gentle pats on his neck, leaning forward to avoid the overhanging rock and frowning curiously towards the dark mouth of the mythical cave. 'There was something weird about those eyes carved into the rock!' she whispered. 'Like they followed you when you moved. Whenever you turned around, they were watching you!'

'Spoo-ooky!' Kirstie grinned. But she was too busy watching out for the paint to pay much attention.

The herd reached the lake and split into smaller groups, ranging themselves along the shore to drink. Soon they were all able to make out the young black-and-white mare, not far from the entrance to the big cave. She was about twenty yards from the water, taking refuge in the shade of the overhang where the primitive drawings had been etched into the rock.

'That's lucky!' Wayne breathed, raising his finger in a warning for the girls not to make any hasty moves. 'Let them settle in,' he advised.

So they watched from behind their screen of aspens as the horses drank. There was a great sucking up of water and gentle strolling through the shallows. Then one or two of the younger horses decided on a roll in the clear water, keeling over on to their sides and revelling in the cool sensation of being submerged. With their bellies turned up and their legs poking into the air, they looked clumsy and comical – nothing like their normal, smooth, elegant selves. Then they struggled back on to their feet, manes and tails dripping, coats bright and freshly washed free of dust.

'Neat!' Lisa whispered. 'It's bath day!'

'And time for a swim!' Kirstie pointed to two brave souls who had taken to the deeper water further out from the shore. Only their heads showed above the surface, while underneath their legs made strong strokes which moved them swiftly away from the herd.

Wayne narrowed his eyes, waiting for precisely the right moment to isolate the paint, who was still taking things easy by the entrance to the cave. The alpha mare was standing about fifty yards further on along the shore, keeping a wary eye on the swimmers as well as watching out for intruders. When she trotted in amongst the paddlers, rounding them up as if to move them on, he inched Prince forward.

'It's now or never!' he murmured. 'The plan is to keep her backed up against that heap of boulders while the rest of the herd takes off. Kirstie, you take the far side, I'll take the middle, and Lisa, stick to the near side. OK?'

They nodded and got ready to launch themselves out of the trees while the paint horse had her back to them. Surprise was their only weapon, and once they'd managed to cut the horse away from the herd it would all be down to patience and stamina.

The three riders exploded from their hiding place in unison, galloping down the hill towards the cave.

The white mare reacted in an instant, gathering the mustangs and setting off along the shore. The rest jostled and stumbled out of the water, anxious not to be left behind.

Meanwhile, the chosen paint whirled around. When she saw Wayne and the girls charging towards her, she reared up, her mane flying, her front hooves pawing the air. Then she was down again, intent on sprinting after the herd.

But Kirstie had already pushed Fresno on to cut off the paint's escape. She reined her horse round to come face to face with the mustang, while Wayne and Lisa took up position.

Trapped! The wild look in the little paint's eyes said it all. While the rest of her two-hundred-strong band took to their heels, she was looking at disaster.

Three riders, three horses forming a semi-circle around her, backing her up against the heap of boulders. She reared again and gave a shrill, frightened whinny.

But Wayne, Kirstie and Lisa didn't give ground. However much the paint panicked, they had to try and contain her, or drive her away from the direction which the herd had taken.

'Easy!' Wayne murmured, holding Prince steady.

'If you work fast, you can drop a rope around her neck!' Lisa urged, until Wayne reminded her that this wasn't the way he worked.

'Yeah, and drag her all the way back to Squaw Lake kickin' up a storm! That way she takes weeks longer to learn to trust me. No, the idea is to run with her, remember!'

Saying this, he eased his horse back and offered the paint a way out, pointing west.

The little mare took it like a shot, launching herself through the gap and making a run down to the shore. Then she pounded off along the pebbles in a mad dash to rid herself of the human threat.

Kirstie, Lisa and Wayne were on her tail, determined not to let her make a U-turn. Forced along the side of the lake, the paint took to the water, splashing up to her hocks and raising a million droplets of spray which flashed all the colours of the rainbow in the sun.

Tucked in behind, Kirstie took the full force of the sudden splash and shivered when the water soaked through her shirt. Running alongside, Wayne and Lisa encouraged her to stay with the paint.

But the wild horse had other ideas. If the only way to shake off her pursuers was by swimming across Great Bird Lake, then swim she would!

She struck out to her left. Soon she was swimming wide of Wayne and Lisa to her right and gaining ground on Fresno and Kirstie.

'OK, here we go!' Kirstie muttered, reining Fresno to the left. They swam across the wake left by the paint, heading her off and pushing her back towards the shore.

'Way to go, Kirstie!' Lisa yelled.

She nodded and raised one arm to put extra pressure on the mustang. 'Git back!' she yelled, cutting in towards her.

The paint veered away from her, spotted the welcoming committee on the shore, then zig-zagged back towards Kirstie.

Her head was pushing through the water, mane

flowing behind. The rest of her body was dimly visible, front legs paddling and flaring outwards, propelling her fast.

Once again, Kirstie and Fresno met the challenge and forced her back, while Wayne drew Lisa away from the shoreline, inviting the fleeing horse to touch dry land.

The tactic worked. Seeing that her escape route across the lake was cut off, the paint made for the pebbles, emerging from the water in a dripping rush and clattering on to the stones before setting off again at a gallop. She raised her front legs high, Spanish style, and arched her proud neck, determined to throw Wayne and Lisa off.

As Fresno swam for the shore, Kirstie watched the two of them take up the challenge. They matched the mustang's powerful, flowing gait, keeping close by her side and eating up the ground.

When Kirstie and Fresno hit the shore, she gave him a couple of seconds to shake himself and gather his wind. She herself was soaked from head to toe, but exhilarated by the experience of swimming in the fresh, clean water. 'Let's go!' she whispered to the sorrel. He responded with a gutsy, all-out gallop to catch the others.

'Look at this paint go!' Lisa turned in the saddle, her face lit up by the thrill of the chase.

'Yeah, tell me that in two hours' time!' Wayne muttered. He was riding with long stirrups, sitting well back in the saddle and in complete harmony with Prince's rangy gallop. 'These mustangs are tough – they'll go for hours without feelin' it!'

'Now he tells us!' Lisa groaned.

'This is gonna be a long day!' Kirstie sighed, her wet, blonde hair flapping against her shoulders. 'Hey, Wayne, we're gonna have to cut her off before she reaches Mary Ellen Black's fence line!'

'Gotcha!' came the snatched reply. 'No problem. We've got thirty miles this side of Hope Valley to work with.'

So, Kirstie thought, *we run the paint across this plateau, north, south, east and west, until she tires!*

This, after all, was what the Native American tribes had done, once the Spanish conquistadors of the sixteenth century had released horses on to the great plains. They'd seen the mustangs roaming wild and recognised in them a way to improve their hunting and fighting skills. The Navahos and the Shoshonis, the Cherokees and the Paiutes had picked out horses from the roaming herds and tamed them to their needs. Then the white man had come in from the east and done the same thing, capturing the 'mestengos' and putting them to work to draw wagons and ploughs and to carry cowboys on long, hard cattle trails.

Paints and Appaloosas had been the native tribes' favourite colours, maybe for the camouflage they gave against the dappled, shadowy landscape. And now here she was, Kirstie Scott, doing what they'd done at least two centuries earlier – tracking and riding down a wild horse, waiting for the creature to submit.

She looked ahead at the dazzling desert. Heat haze was already forming and making the horizon shimmer; there wasn't a scrap of shelter anywhere. Kirstie envisaged how she would feel after two, four, or maybe even six hours of this. The temperature would rise, the sun would bake the land, and the wild horse could still be running.

'Crazy!' Lisa murmured with a shake of her head.

'Yeah!' Kirstie grinned, settling into Fresno's smooth, rhythmical gallop. The quarter-horse was nowhere near as pretty as the paint, but he was a determined, gutsy guy. 'Like I said, this is gonna be a long, hard day!'

3

It was three in the afternoon and they were still running.

'She's a tough little lady,' Wayne grunted, settling Prince into a lope some ten yards behind the paint.

'And smart!' Kirstie added. They'd chased the mustang fifteen miles west, almost within sight of the Hope Valley fence line. Then the three riders had cut the paint off and turned her south, running parallel with the foothills across open country.

They would be watching her closely, trying to

pick up signals that the race was almost run. That would be when her head went down close to the ground and her mouth began to work in a circular, grinding motion, as if to say, 'OK, you win. I'm ready to talk turkey!'

Sometimes the body language made them think it was about to happen and they would ease up to give the mare space to think about things. Then all of a sudden she would put on an extra burst of speed down a draw where it was difficult to follow. Her head would be up, knowing that she'd outsmarted them and they would have to crash through scrub oak and catch her up, ready to begin over.

'She's bred to do this, it's in her genetic make-up,' Wayne explained. He and the girls had criss-crossed the plain, following hard on the heels of the paint, their own horses working willingly for them. 'She only knows flight – it's her means of survival.'

'How come she can travel so far?' a weary Lisa gasped. 'For a small horse, she sure has stamina!'

'It's down to her feet,' Wayne told her, sending Kirstie to gallop ahead and cut across the paint's track.

'Her feet?' Lisa echoed.

'Yeah. Day after day, week after week for years on end she's been running over rock and hard ground. Those feet are tougher than any leather soles we might wear. That's how come she can run and run.'

A neat piece of teamwork between Wayne, Kirstie and Lisa then turned the horse eastwards, back towards Great Bird Lake where the chase had begun. Now the sun was on their shoulders and backs, burning down from an intense blue sky. On the vast, open plain they were the only visible creatures, raising dust and galloping on.

'I know something,' Lisa grumbled. 'If that mustang doesn't die of thirst in the next thirty minutes, then I sure will!'

'That's why we turned her towards the lake,' Wayne said.

'Call me party pooper, but how many guys have been killed trying to break a wild mustang?' Lisa asked.

'Jeez!' Kirstie muttered under her breath. Her shirt was wet with sweat, her lips dry. Every bone in her body ached after five or six hours of pursuit.

'Plenty,' Wayne answered. 'The most dangerous

part of a mustang is his front feet. They can give you a sock in the jaw that'll bust your teeth clean out of your head.'

'Ouch!' Lisa grimaced.

'Yeah, thanks for asking, Lisa!' Still watching every tiny move made by the paint, Kirstie noted that the last manoeuvre had worked and they were now definitely headed towards the lake.

'That's why, at Squaw Lake we don't break mustangs. That'd be like ridin' the Wall of Death. What we do is gentle them along – no rough stuff. We don't wanna crush their spirit, but we do want to work alongside them and get their co-operation.'

'Yeah, I like that – in theory!' Lisa gave a tired laugh. 'The only problem is, our little friend doesn't know the meaning of the word.'

Despite her aching body, Kirstie didn't for a moment want to give up the chase. The fluid, fast movement of the paint in flight, her perfect balance that allowed her to change direction in a split second, her strength and wildness, were all incredible to watch. Kirstie figured that in a way it would be a shame when the mustang finally gave in, as Wayne said she would.

Now they were approaching the crumbling cave dwellings and the long, clear stretch of water. A cooler breeze came off the lake and gave the riders and their horses some relief from the afternoon heat.

The wild horse must have felt the same let-up from the stifling dust and sun. She eased her pace as she reached the cliffs, obviously ready to take on water. Cautiously picking a way down to the water's edge that wouldn't trap her against any rocks, she trotted foward, lowered her head and drank.

At this point, the temptation for Wayne and the girls to ride forward and rope the mare was at its greatest.

It'd be so easy! Kirstie thought. *One second, and the lasso would be round her neck!*

But Wayne read her mind. 'No way!' he whispered.

The mustang saw that her pursuers were not about to make any move. She relaxed and drank some more, cast a curious look in their direction, seeming to toy with the idea of making a shy approach. But then she darted away, fifty yards along the shore.

'She's playing a game with us!' Lisa exclaimed.

Wayne grinned. 'She sure is less edgy than she was. She may even be foolin' with us, like you say.'

Kirstie thought hard, watching how glad the mare was to be sucking up water. 'I figure she's grateful to us for letting her drink. She's comfortable with having us around too.'

'Almost ready to join us, huh?' Wayne considered his next tactic. The mustang was definitely calm and easy now, letting them know that their stubborn pursuit no longer bothered her so much as it had. 'Wait here,' Wayne told the girls.

Smoothly and slowly he rode Prince down to the water, edging closer to the mustang. His quarter-horse drank noisily and the paint looked up. Wayne edged closer still, then gave her eye contact, which sent her skittering back. He too withdrew to a safe distance.

'Now we have a new game,' Lisa sighed. 'What did Wayne gain by that?'

Kirstie shrugged. 'At least the paint didn't kick up her heels and disappear over the horizon!'

Wayne was now fifty yards from the mustang, who stood alert but not scared.

'OK, we're almost there,' Wayne promised,

calling for Lisa and Kirstie to join him. 'See how her ear is on us, and how her head is goin' down.'

'Finally!' Lisa gave an exhausted sigh.

'She knows she can't shake off the pressure by runnin', and what she needs to do is make friends. I'll ride up to her on Prince a couple more times, then back off for a while. The time after that, she should be happy for me to ride right up and touch her.'

So the girls crossed their fingers and watched Wayne make his approach – once, twice, and then three times. By then, the mare was itching to follow him to find out more, stretching out her lowered head and tottering a few steps after him.

'OK, this is it!' Wayne murmured on approach number four. He rode quietly up to the paint, who still hugged the water's edge, going close enough to sidle up alongside her. He sat easily, waiting a few moments before he reached out and stroked the mare's neck.

'Oh, wow!' Lisa breathed.

Kirstie felt a surge of pure joy. 'That's amazing!'

The mustang had accepted the man's touch.

'The next step is where I hang this loose rope round your neck,' Wayne said in a low voice, gently

unhitching the coil from his saddle horn.

The movement startled the mustang, but she stayed at his side.

'You won't like it much, but you have to trust me, OK?' He slipped the noose over her head and waited for her to run.

'Go on, scoot!' he encouraged, setting the mare off into a lope through the shallow water. Securing the end of the rope round his saddle horn, he urged Prince to follow her.

'Crazy!' Lisa cried out in dismay. 'What is Wayne doin'?'

'Driving her off in order to make her come back to him.' Kirstie knew enough about the methods used in a round pen to realise that an unschooled horse pretty soon learned to accept a rope as long as he trusted and respected the guy who had attached it to him. This trust was the bottom line, and she knew that Wayne had done enough through eight hours of riding to earn it.

Sure enough, the mustang soon left off resisting the rope. She'd only run a couple of hundred yards before she let up and agreed for Wayne and Prince to lead her back.

'Hmm,' Lisa grunted. 'I wish I understood what goes on inside a horse's head.'

Kirstie gazed at the three dripping figures who came towards them. Broad-shouldered Wayne sat upright in the saddle wearing a proud smile. Prince, his coat black after the soaking he'd received in the lake, ambled steadily. And then astonishingly, the paint followed on the end of a rope without any objection, head up, ears pricked and quite easy with what had happened.

The girls fell silent as the trio drew near. This was the horse they'd admired from a distance over so many miles, coming up to them with her high-stepping walk, looking curiously at them with her enormous, dark-brown eyes.

'Go ahead, touch her,' Wayne invited.

So Kirstie stepped forward and reached out her hand. She laid it on the mustang's wet neck, then ran it down her withers and along her flank. 'You're a little honey,' she murmured. 'A real beauty!'

'Chiquitita,' Lisa added with a beaming smile. 'Our special little girl!'

'We dallied her all the way back to Squaw Lake!' Kirstie told her mom on the phone. It was Friday morning, and after a good sleep she was busting to tell the people back home about their achievement of the day before.

'Good job, honey. It sounds like you had a real neat time. Who was the dally horse?'

'First off it was Prince. He's a steady guy, so the mustang soon settled in. Then Wayne gave Lisa a turn with Snowbird, then finally me on Fresno. It felt fantastic to be guiding her into a new life back at Squaw Lake, where we know for sure that she'll get four diamond treatment!'

'Sounds like you really fell for that horse in a big

way,' Sandy Scott laughed. 'But hey, why am I surprised?'

'Listen, Mom, she's so beautiful. Lisa gave her a Spanish name – Chiquitita – and it's kinda stuck. Now we're hoping that Rob likes her as much as we all do.'

'Will you two girls be able to tear yourselves away next week when your visit is over?'

'Gee, it'll be hard,' Kirstie admitted. 'Mom, you can't imagine how brilliant the wild horses are. You see the whole herd and it just blows you away!'

'So our tame ramuda of plain old quarter-horses has lost its attraction, huh?' Sandy was teasing, but at the same time sounded a touch wistful.

Kirstie brought to mind the string of horses at Half-Moon Ranch. She pictured Johnny Mohawk and Rodeo Rocky, her brother's horse, Cadillac, and her very own Lucky. 'No way!' she protested. 'I love them all to pieces.'

'Yeah, and they're all doin' fine,' her mom assured her. 'Listen honey, I mean it, have a good time out there with Wayne and Rob. You have one more week before you get on the plane back to Colorado Springs, so make the most of every minute, OK!'

'We sure will.' Glancing out of the kitchen window, Kirstie spotted a Jeep pulling into the yard. 'It looks like Rob just got back from San Francisco. Mom, I gotta go. Bye!'

After a hurried farewell, she dashed outside to greet Wayne's son.

Rob Raburn was a fourteen-year-old replica of his dad, Wayne. He shared the family light-grey eyes and dark hair and was growing tall and strong. He also had the same quiet, laid-back manner which could fool you into thinking he was shy, until, if the subject was horses, he opened his mouth and spoke with a down-to-earth confidence. After two weeks in his company, Lisa and Kirstie found they could kid around with him like an older brother.

'Hey Rob, how did it go?' Lisa got there before Kirstie, her freckled face smothered in sunblock and wearing a long-sleeved sweatshirt and light trousers. Her usual baseball cap was jammed firmly over her short auburn hair.

'Not so good,' he admitted, taking a bag from Walter, who had driven him in from the airport.

Wayne's assistant went about slamming car doors with his usual abruptness before disappearing into the house.

'We heard your grandpa was ill,' Kirstie said quietly, noting the small frown lines between Rob's dark eyebrows.

He nodded. 'It turns out it's serious. They took him to the hospital and put him in the cardiac unit. Grandma says it's his heart they're worried about.'

By this time, Wayne had come out into the yard. He took a long look at his worried son. 'Hey,' he said, low-key as ever. 'I got a call from your mom early this mornin'. She gave me the lowdown.'

Rob shot him an anxious glace. 'Did she say that they thought Gramps would make it?'

Wayne sighed. 'I'd be lyin' if I said yes, son. The doctors put his chances at fifty-fifty.'

Taking a deep breath which choked in his throat, Rob nodded. 'Maybe I should turn around and fly back,' he murmured.

But his dad laid a hand on his arm. 'Not right now. Mom says to give it another couple of days at least. She's taking care of Grandma and the hospital is one of the best in California. She wants you to stay here at Squaw Lake until they have more news.'

Lisa glanced at Kirstie. 'Bummer!' she muttered under her breath.

'Yeah. The new horse doesn't make up for this hospital stuff, does it?' Kirstie whispered.

But Wayne knew his son inside out and he chose this down-hearted moment to take Rob straight out to the arena to show him Chiquitita.

Rob wasn't expecting anything good, and from the back his manner looked downbeat, tired and empty. It wasn't until he reached the arena fence that he really began to take in his surroundings.

The round enclosure stood half in the full glare of the morning sun, half in deep shadow, its sandy surface churned up by a horse who had been racing round the circuit for some time. As they arrived at the fence, a black-and-white blur burst out of the shade, galloping, bucking and kicking her way round the arena. Her head and tail were up, Arabian style, adrenalin pumping big time through her sleek, fluid body.

Rob's eyes opened wide, his jaw dropped but he said nothing.

'New little mare,' Wayne commented, non-committal. 'What d'you think?'

Rob took in the perfect conformation, the proud

light in the eye, the showy display of strength and willpower. 'Cool,' he breathed.

'The girls and me dallied her in from Great Bird Lake yesterday,' his dad told him, as if they'd driven down to the local store to buy ice-cream.

Yeah, after eight hours of sweat and aching muscles! Kirstie thought.

Three times round the arena, the paint mare galloped and showed off.

'Hmm. Good job.' Still Rob eyed the horse warily, not quite sure where she fitted in with his dad's management of the wild herd. But he was definitely fascinated by the new arrival, climbing on to the bottom rung of the fence and watching her run.

'She goes by the name of Chiquitita,' Wayne went on. 'Lisa chose it. We think it kinda fits.'

'Yeah.'

'So what's your opinion? D'you like her?'

Rob nodded. 'She's a handful.'

'How big a handful?' Wayne turned his full attention to Rob, studying his face closely. 'D'you reckon Walter could gentle her, for instance?'

A quick shake of the head followed, but Rob didn't speak.

'No, me neither. I figure she needs an expert.'

'Well then, it's down to you, Dad.' Eyes glued on the mustang, Rob still didn't expect what came next.

Wayne sized him up and down. 'I was hopin' you might take her on, son,' he said quietly. 'D'you think you could put some willingness and co-operation inside that pretty head of hers?'

Kirstie and Lisa watched Rob slowly tear his eyes off Chiquitita to stare at his father. 'Me?' he whispered.

'Yeah, you,' Wayne insisted, still acting like he'd brought home a small treat from the grocery store. Then his face broke into a wide grin. 'Rob, if you want her, she's yours!'

4

'We spent a whole day in the baking desert to fetch
you this horse!' Lisa laid it on thick for Rob's
benefit. 'We galloped so hard, we got sore . . . well,
sore everythin'!'

'Across endless plains, defying Mary Ellen
Black's gun-slingers, plunging into the ice-cold
depths of Great Bird Lake . . .' Kirstie took up the
theme as she, Lisa and Rob put their feet up at the
end of Rob's first day of working with Chiquitita.
The girls sat on the porch swing while Rob
straddled the rail and leaned back against an
upright support post.

'. . . Yeah, daring the nasty old Water Baby to sneak out and grab us. We were nearly lyin' on the bed of that lake, bones picked clean by the serpent. And all for you, Rob Raburn!'

'Well I sure do appreciate that,' he grinned. He swung his leg free of the rail and went down on one knee. 'In fact, girls, I don't know how I'm ever gonna repay you!'

'Oh yuck, Rob, you're actin' like some wimpy Romeo! Get up off the floor!' Lisa squirmed.

'Why? What's the problem? I'm only tryin' to say thanks!'

As Rob fooled around on his knees, Wayne's assistant, Walter Gray, walked brusquely across the yard and into the house without acknowledging them.

Lisa raised her eyebrows behind his back. 'What's up with that!'

Rob shrugged and got to his feet. 'Yeah, Walter ain't exactly the most talkative guy around.'

'So anyway, how d'you like working with Chiquitita?' Kirstie swung the conversation back on to her favourite subject. She and Lisa had watched two long sessions, morning and then afternoon.

At first, Rob had simply spent time in the arena with the paint mare, letting her get used to the idea of contact with yet another human, and this time a boy on foot, minus his horse. It had been a novel idea for Chiquitita and she'd been shy at first, but then curiosity had finally got the better of her and she'd made the approach. Rob had made contact by a series of gentle rubs and strokes, taking his time and not trying any work with ropes or halters.

'That was me saying hi,' he'd explained after two and a half hours in the arena with his wild mustang.

'I've heard of long goodbyes,' Lisa had commented. 'But never such a long hello!'

Then, in the afternoon, Rob had moved on to the next phase. Chiquitita had fed and drunk, and had been lying down in the sun when he'd ridden quietly into the arena on a steady, grey gelding called Moonpie, carrying a surcingle with him.

'This is to get her used to the idea of a cinch under her belly,' he'd told Lisa and Kirstie.

'Are you sure she's ready?' Kirstie had asked nervously. She'd been afraid that moving on too fast would spook the mustang and set her way back.

But Rob's judgement had been good. He and

Moonpie had worked alongside Chiquitita, eventually slipping the surcingle down the far side of the mustang and using a hook to catch the dangling end, then bringing the girth up under her belly.

Chiquitita had kicked out with her front legs, but then accepted the strap and been happy to move from a walk into a trot beside Moonpie. Lisa and Kirstie had given a small cheer and the mare had responded by breaking into a beautiful smooth lope, showing off her grace and speed.

So really, Kirstie knew that her question as they sat on the porch in the evening sun, was redundant. 'How d'you like working with Chiquitita?' was like asking Rob, 'Do you need air to breathe?'

Rob planned ahead. 'Tomorrow's Saturday. I figure I can try her with a light saddle and a bridle.'

'Already?' Lisa's eyes lit up. 'Hey, you make sure not to do it without us, OK!'

He grinned and nodded. He put on a long Texan drawl. 'I'll move heaven and earth to fit in with your schedule, Miss Lisa! What time will you have done with breakfast?'

Before she could invent a reply, their talk was

interrupted by raised voices from inside the house.

'I want this transfer now,' Walter was insisting. 'I ain't sticking around this God-forsaken spot until New Year.'

Kirstie, Lisa and Rob exchanged glances. It sounded like Wayne's assistant had come out of his shell in a big way.

'Your contract says you work with me here at Squaw Lake until the end of the year,' Wayne insisted more quietly. 'Sure I know it's kinda quiet, but I laid out the conditions when I hired you. Nobody tried to fool you into thinkin' this was a glamorous life.'

'But there's no stinkin' place for a guy to relax and chill out with other guys. All I'm askin' is for an early transfer to Pia Apo Gulch, then I can get into town of an evenin'.'

'Sorry, Walter, I can't do that.'

'Why the heck not? You got Rob here with you to help out until September. Once those girls have hightailed it out of here, the kid can fix his mind back on the job. And after that you can have any one of half a dozen guys that the Bureau could send to take my place.'

'Rob is fourteen years old,' Wayne reminded

him. 'He may be good around the horses, but he's not old enough to be officially employed.'

'Yeah but he's old enough to have his very own mustang,' Walter sneered. 'Did anyone mention that to the Bureau of Land Management, I wonder?'

'That's enough!' Wayne snapped back. 'The bottom line is, I gave you a job through to the end of the year. Come next January, you get your transfer to work with Rocky Stewart at Pia Apo, as we wrote into the contract.'

Listening in from the porch, Lisa and Kirstie grimaced.

'I never did like that guy!' Kirstie whispered.

Lisa agreed. 'He goes around starin' at you like you just murdered his brother! And he never talks!'

'He's talkin' now,' Rob muttered before striding off across the yard, unwilling to listen to any more.

And it was true – Walter still hadn't taken no for an answer. 'I don't like the way you figure it,' he was insisting. 'If you don't want the Bureau to send in a new guy, there's hands at Pia Apo who'd change places with me, no problem. Take Joseph Secola, for instance. That guy's Shoshoni through and through. He knows this Basin area better'n I do. Why not bring him in?'

'Because Joseph has a wife and family livin' near Tamapo, and you don't have folks to take care of.' With his patience stretched to the limit, Wayne made one last effort to reason with Walter. 'Besides, you need four more months to learn the basics of herd management before you transfer to the ranch.'

'Don't give me that, Wayne. I already learned all I need to know about these wild horses. I'm ready to move on, I tell you!'

There was a silence, then a scraping of a chair back from the kitchen table as Wayne stood up. 'The answer's no, Walter. N-O, no. Get it?'

Another chair scraped across the floor. 'Yessir!' Walter spat out.

'Quick, let's get out of here!' Kirstie hissed. She didn't want to be in Walter's way when he stormed out.

So she and Lisa vaulted the rail and scooted off around the side of the house. They heard the door swing open and Walter's footsteps stamp across the porch. Risking a backwards glance, they caught sight of his thin, glowering face.

'Man, he should thank his lucky stars he still has a job!' Lisa whispered.

Kirstie nodded. 'Mom always says that the type of help you hire either makes or breaks a place. Half-Moon Ranch has the best hands you could ever hope to find.'

'Well, I feel sorry for Wayne. He deserves better.' She glowered after the tall, skinny figure who had just vanished into the barn.

'Forget him,' Kirstie advised. 'I'm more worried about Rob and his grandpa. Let's go keep him company, see if we can stop him from losin' too much sleep.'

They found Rob round the back of the barn, gazing out in the direction of Thunder Rock. The tall landmark wasn't visible until you rode on to the flat plain beyond the rim of Squaw Lake Basin. Like Water Cave to the north, it had gathered many Native American myths over the years. The one that stuck in Kirstie's mind was the tale that identified the rock as a sacred Shoshoni site where young braves would go on vision quests. They would fast by the rock for days, seeking advice from the Great Spirit. Then they would return to their tribes full of wisdom and the courage to face their enemies in battle.

'Remember when we found El Dorado by Thunder Rock?' Kirstie murmured to Rob.

El Dorado – the black stallion, proud protector of the wild herd. It was there, under the deep ledge on the sacred site, that they'd tracked him down and treated his injuries.

Rob sighed and nodded. 'Y'know, the Shoshonis were lucky people. When they were in trouble they always knew who to pray to.'

'Yeah, I know what you mean.' Kirstie gazed across the desert, watching pink begin to tinge the gold of the western sky.

There was a long silence, broken only by the muffled breathing and shuffling of the saddle horses in their stalls.

'You gotta think positive about your grandpa,' Lisa urged Rob quietly.

He nodded. Without looking at them, he described the scene he'd left in the city. 'The last time I saw Gramps in the hospital, he was hooked up to a hundred tubes and machines. The poor old guy could hardly move. The nurses were reading screens and writing stuff on charts.

Gramps looked kinda lost. And small – like he'd suddenly shrunk.'

The hesitant account made a lump come into Kirstie's throat. 'Lisa's right. You have to picture him getting through this.'

'I'm tryin'.' Rob took a deep breath. 'Some of the time it works. Like when I'm workin' with Chiquitita. I don't forget about Gramps, but my mind is up and I'm thinkin' he can lick this problem and get back to bein' how he was before it happened. He'll be out there playin' golf with his buddies, crackin' jokes.

'But when I'm away from Chiquitita, like now, all the bad stuff comes pourin' in. It's as if something is chokin' me and stoppin' me from breathin' the air, and I'm picturin' him hooked up to all those tubes, lookin' lost and old and just wantin' to give in.'

'Hold it!' Kirstie told him sternly. 'Did your grandpa ever give up on anything in his entire life?'

Rob shot her a quick look. 'No, I guess not.'

Her shrewd guess had paid off. 'He's not a quitter?'

'No way.'

'So why would he start quittin' now?'

He nodded. 'Right.' After another silence, he turned all the way around to face the girls. 'I definitely need to go back to San Francisco,' he decided.

'Tomorrow?' Lisa asked.

Kirstie's first thought was, *What will happen to Chiquitita?*

'No. I figure it'll be Monday. That means I can work two days with my horse, but after that I need you to promise that you'll take over. If you do, I won't feel bad about leavin' her so soon.'

Kirstie gasped. 'You don't even have to ask!' she assured him.

'And don't worry, while you're away we'll take excellent care of her!' Lisa swore.

'We're here until the end of next week. Will you be back before we leave?' Kirstie asked.

Rob nodded. 'I hope.'

'So we'll call you every day in San Francisco with a detailed report,' Lisa told him. 'If Chiquitita so much as sneezes, we'll be on the phone askin' your advice!'

Managing to smile, Rob told them it was a deal. 'You don't reckon I'm makin' too big a thing?' he asked.

'Hey, if my grandpa was ill, I'd be the first one on that plane!' Lisa assured him.

Kirstie said nothing, remembering sadly how her own grandparents had both died within a year of each other and left Half-Moon Ranch to their daughter, Sandy, Kirstie's mom.

'Thanks.' Pulling himself up and squaring his shoulders, Rob said he would go and talk to his dad right then.

Lisa linked arms with Kirstie and watched him stride off around the side of the barn. 'Let's go check the horses,' she suggested quietly.

They slipped into the barn through a back door, glad to find some cool shade. The sweet smell of stacked bales of alfalfa greeted them and they lingered for a while amongst rows of tack hanging from hooks, enjoying the way narrow rays of sunlight played on the metal bits and picked up dancing specks of dust.

Then a slammed door made them realise they weren't alone in the barn. They saw Walter emerge from a stall and shoot the bolt shut behind him. The horse inside the stall whinnied nervously as the man stamped on down the row.

'Jeez, that guy!' Lisa muttered through gritted teeth.

Wayne's assistant was evidently still in a foul mood after his disagreement with his boss. Without noticing Kirstie and Lisa, he seized the handles of a nearby barrow which was laden with used straw from one of the stalls. His rough handling made the barrow tip on its side, spilling its contents on the dirt floor. Swearing, he forked the wet straw back into the barrow, kicking stray wisps to one side. Then he took the fork into the next stall.

'Git back!'

The girls heard Walter snap at the horse and saw a startled sorrel head appear over the stall door.

'That's Fresno!' Kirstie whispered with a frown. She pictured Walter shoving his weight around inside the confined space. She didn't like to think of the spikes from Walter's fork going anywhere near the gelding's legs. In this frame of mind, the ranch hand wouldn't be too particular.

'I said, git back!' came the snarling voice a second time. Then there was a thud and Fresno drew back from the door.

'You want me to hog-tie you?' Walter threatened. 'Or will this headcollar keep you out of my hair?'

Presumably he managed to sling on the halter and tie the rope tight against the wall because the horse didn't reappear while he cleaned out the stall. There was more barging and thudding, some swearing, and then a high, frightened whinny from Fresno.

'C'mon!' Kirstie frowned. She strode down the barn determined to see exactly what was going on.

When she and Lisa reached Fresno's stall, Walter had his back turned and was jabbing at the gelding with the pitchfork. 'Stupid horse!' he muttered. 'Can't you stand and let me work?'

Fresno skittered away from the sharp prongs, but the rope stopped him from moving far. The more Walter jabbed, the more agitated the horse became.

'Let me hold him for you!' Kirstie broke in, going quickly into the stall.

Walter spun round, a guilty look in his eye. Then he covered up quick as a flash. 'Darned horse just kicked out at me for no reason!'

'Yeah well, whatever happened he's acting pretty spooked. Why don't I lead him out into the yard, calm him down for you?'

Reluctantly Walter stepped aside. 'This horse has a mean streak. You can't turn your back for a second.'

Still frowning, Kirstie untied Fresno. As soon as the rope was loose, he backed away, then reared up and made a quick dash for the door. The rope slipped through Kirstie's hands and she yelled at Lisa for her to stop the horse.

'See!' Walter acted as if his point had just been proven.

'Got him!' Lisa yelled. 'Hey, there's a cut across his knee! It's bleedin'!'

'Take him on out. I'll follow.' Kirstie glared at Walter, who shrugged. 'Don't look at me,' he muttered, turning his back and getting on with his chore of mucking out the stall.

'Fresno didn't have a cut on his leg last time I looked!' Kirstie insisted.

'Yeah, stupid horse just kicked out at the wall and smashed his knee against the wood partition.'

Walter's angry excuse wouldn't have fooled a three-year-old kid, Kirstie thought. In fact, she'd have bet big money that the cut had been made by the sharp prongs of the fork. But how did she challenge him without calling him a liar to his face?

So she sighed and beat a retreat.

Sure enough, when she joined Lisa, she saw that there was a raw wound across Fresno's front right knee. 'Walter says he kicked the wall,' she said in a flat tone of disbelief.

'Yeah!' Gingerly dabbing at the cut, Lisa discovered that it wasn't deep. 'Good boy,' she murmured.

'So what do we tell Wayne?' Kirstie wondered.

'You don't tell him anything!' Walter had come up silently and made them jump. He stared angrily at them. 'I tell the boss that the horse caught his leg on this nail which was sticking out of the wall.'

Kirstie and Lisa looked hard at the shiny nail which Walter held up in front of them. Both their faces told him what they thought of his pathetic lie.

'You plannin' on tellin' him somethin' different?' he scowled.

Kirstie grabbed Fresno's lead-rope and held tight this time. 'Maybe!' she answered, swallowing hard.

'Yeah well, think again,' Walter sneered. ' 'Cos I'd deny everythin' you tried to tell him. And without witnesses, you can't prove a darned thing!'

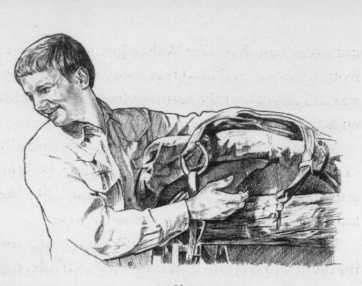

5

'I so hate that guy!' Lisa's helpless outburst about Walter Gray expressed the way Kirstie felt too.

They came across him first thing next morning, talking with Wayne in the yard as the girls went eagerly to find Rob. It was time to begin another session in the arena with Chiquitita.

'Wayne didn't believe that stupid story about the nail,' Kirstie muttered as they hurried by. 'He knows perfectly well that his stalls are in good order and no way would there be a big ugly nail sticking out for a horse to tear its leg on!'

'Yeah, and did you see it? It was brand new –

not even bent. I reckon Walter just grabbed one from a toolbox and used it as a lame excuse!' Lisa was still angry that the assistant had got away with an act of blatant cruelty.

'Maybe we should tell Wayne what we actually saw.' Kirstie slowed down before they reached the arena. 'Then again, where's our evidence, like the lowdown pond life pointed out at the time?'

'Hmm.' For at least the tenth time since the incident, Lisa joined Kirstie in considering whether or not they'd done the right thing. 'I figure Wayne would believe us. For a start, what reason would we have to lie?'

'Hey, girls!' Rob interrupted, bright and breezy. He was heading for the small paddock down by Squaw Lake where Chiquitita had spent the night. 'I changed my mind about workin' in the arena. Let's try the lakeside instead.'

'Why? What's the difference?' Dropping the tricky subject of Walter Gray, Kirstie followed Rob into the barn.

'It's cooler down by the water, and it feels more like home to her. Besides, down there no one will interfere with the work. We'll have peace and quiet.'

'Sounds good,' Lisa agreed, taking a saddle pad, bridle and surcingle from him.

Kirstie caught sight of the saddle pad and then the small kiddie saddle which Rob picked up and gave to her. 'Hey, does this mean what I think it means?' she asked, her eyes lighting up.

He nodded. 'We're movin' on from surcingle to saddle.' Grabbing a full-size stock saddle, he took its weight and led the way out of the barn. 'If things go smoothly, I'll be up on Chiquitita's back and ridin' her before the end of the day!'

The enclosure by the lake took a breeze from the water which rippled the surface and rustled gently through the long, dry grass. The light was dazzling, the sky as blue as ever.

Chiquitita was waiting for them. She stood to attention, watching with interest as Kirstie and Rob slung the two saddles over the fence. These were strange contraptions to her – more objects to work out and slide into place in her simple, wild view of the world. After looking at them for a few minutes, she walked up to them and gave them a close inspection.

'What beats me is how fast all this is happenin','

Kirstie murmured, watching the little paint mare sniff and begin to tug at the edges of the saddles with her teeth. 'Forty-eight hours ago, she was runnin' with the herd, totally free. Now look at her!'

Rob grinned as he steadied the stock saddle to prevent it from toppling to the ground. 'Yeah, people make the mistake of believin' it's quicker to use the old way of sackin' out and beatin' a horse into submission. The fact is, the gentle way is a whole lot faster. Once you win their trust, you've made a strong link between you. The rest all just follows on.'

Nodding, Kirstie saw that Rob's beliefs about training a horse fitted in exactly with her own. 'Sure, I know that. I do it at home all the time. But never on a wild mustang. That's my point – Chiquitita is acting like she already belongs to you!'

'Yeah, let's hope,' Rob said as he climbed the fence and jumped into the paddock, holding the surcingle in one hand. Working on foot for the first time, he soon persuaded the mare to accept the strap which he passed under her belly and buckled tight.

'Would you look at that! She hardly even

noticed,' Lisa breathed. The girls leaned on the fence and watched Rob every step of the way.

His next move was to drop a rope over Chiquitita's head. He talked as he worked, showering her with pats and strokes. Then he walked her gently towards their audience, asking Lisa to pass him the saddle pad.

He took away the surcingle and eased the pad on to her back. The unfamiliar feeling surprised her and made her flinch, but she took it without any major complaints.

By this time, Kirstie was completely caught up in the situation which was developing in front of her. For her it held a magic that no other experience came near – she was fascinated by the way the boy and the mustang communicated, and understood that every little move conveyed a meaning.

'We're ready for the kiddie saddle,' Rob called quietly, asking for Kirstie to bring it to him while he stood with Chiquitita by the water's edge.

She carried it calmly and handed it over.

'See this?' Rob allowed the mare to sniff at it once more. 'This is the saddle I used when I was three years old. It's kinda light. I figured you wouldn't mind tryin' this one out.'

Chiquitita examined it closely and turned her head as Rob lifted it on to her back. Before he could lower it, she kicked out and skittered sideways.

'OK, too much too soon,' Rob conceded, giving her some slack on the lead-rope. 'So I'll just lay it on the ground here, and you can sniff at it some more, make sure it ain't gonna dig its claws into you when I put it on your back!'

Marvelling at his patience, Kirstie backed off to her original place next to Lisa.

'Isn't that beautiful!' Lisa breathed. 'No force, no pain – just total understanding!'

As Rob had obviously predicted, Chiquitita soon overcame her suspicion of the small saddle. The second time he tried to place it on her back, she said '*OK, you know best.*'

'Excellent!' Kirstie whispered.

But still not the ultimate goal for the day. Fitting the larger stock saddle was yet to come, and then the biggest test of all, when Rob would become the first person to ride the wild horse.

It took all day. They broke for lunch, leaving

Chiquitita to feed and rest. Wayne asked about their progress and grunted in satisfaction when Kirstie and Lisa went into raptures over the trust that Rob had built up.

'He was amazing!' Lisa told Wayne. 'I never saw him put a single foot wrong!'

'Is that so?' Wayne was keeping Walter waiting as he stopped in the yard to talk with the kids. The two men were due to drive out to Thunder Rock that afternoon to collect some paperwork and equipment stored in a small cabin there. So Walter sat in the Jeep, impatiently tapping the steering wheel while Wayne chatted.

'Later today he hopes to ride her!' Kirstie told him. 'How cool is that!'

'Yeah, pity I won't be here.' Wayne glanced at his son to see him blushing under the praise. 'You choose a good patch of ground for your big moment,' he said with a grin. 'Then if the horse decides that you're puttin' too big a strain on the friendship, at least you can part company without breakin' any bones.'

'Thanks, Dad! He means, if Chiquitita bucks me off, make sure I choose a soft landing!' Rob explained.

'Which I'm sure won't happen!' Lisa said stoutly.

'Well, have fun,' Wayne told them. 'And listen, Rob, I have a bad feelin' that our neighbour, Mary Ellen Black, may drop by later today. I heard she wants to meet with me – some stuff about BLM boundaries. And you know Mary Ellen never makes appointments. If she visits and I'm not back yet, tell her six o'clock.'

Rob took in the message and watched the Jeep pull out of the yard.

'Why does he say he has a *bad* feeling?' Kirstie asked as she, Rob and Lisa went back down to the lake. 'Is she some kind of monster?'

'Wait and see,' Rob advised. 'All I'm sayin' is that Mary Ellen Black makes the giant water serpent of Great Bird Lake look like a tame little pussy cat!'

Lisa winced. 'Remind me to keep a low profile,' she muttered to Kirstie.

Then it was down to work again, this time in a blazing sun without any breeze. Chiquitita trotted up to Rob, looking for someone to talk with after her siesta. He in turn gave her all the pats and rubs that she'd grown to expect.

Quite soon he reintroduced her to the saddle

pad, patting it firmly into place and letting her walk around freely until she forgot it was there.

'Now for the stock saddle,' Kirstie whispered. She answered Rob's signal to take him the heavy tack, then faded quietly into the background.

'OK, so this is bigger,' Rob told Chiquitita. 'It smells the same, but it's gonna weigh a whole lot more.'

The mare sighed and snorted. When he eased the saddle into position, she waited a second, decided she didn't like it and bucked it off. It landed with a thud, stirrups flying.

'Major spook time!' Lisa commented, watching Chiquitita leap clear.

Kirstie noticed that Rob's attitude didn't change. He was still calm and patient, giving the horse some slack, waiting until she was over it.

Twice, then three times, Chiquitita showed her dislike of the full-size saddle. Then on the fourth attempt, she seemed to realise that Rob wasn't about to give up. So she let the weight stay there and lowered her head as if to say, 'You win!'

Rob rewarded her with more rubs across her withers, then he stooped to fasten the cinch. 'How about that bridle now?' he called to Lisa.

She ran with the tack, watched as Rob slid the

snaffle bit into Chiquitita's mouth without a hitch, then backed away.

'This is it!' Kirstie took a deep breath. What might seem to many like a small action of mounting the horse was in fact a miracle about to happen.

Carefully Rob put the toe of his boot into the stirrup.

Chiquitita quivered but stood steady.

Rob lifted himself up and swung his leg over the saddle. The horse shifted slightly, found her balance and settled. Her pricked ears were turned towards Rob, totally focused on what he was doing.

Slowly he lowered himself into a sitting position.

'Yes!' Kirstie whispered. An amazing thing had happened in this moment when a strong, graceful, wild spirit had accepted of her own free will that she would work with and serve her rider.

Chiquitita had carried Rob as if she'd been born to it. She'd been laid-back and easy, walking evenly, then had broken into a steady trot and finally a lope. He had sat deep in the saddle with long stirrups, using the reins lightly to bring about flying lead changes or pull the horse to a stop.

Kirstie and Lisa had loved every second, though

Kirstie did find herself wishing hard that it had been her in the saddle, experiencing those moments first hand. *Maybe some day I'll get to be the first to ride a wild horse!* she told herself. For now it had to be enough to watch Rob bonding with lovely little Chiquitita.

When the session was over, they gathered up the tack and watched the paint mare stand by the water to drink. With the sun low in the sky behind her, she seemed to be surrounded by a pale golden halo, her figure strong and dark, with the white patches standing out in stark contrast.

Kirstie stood by the fence for a while, wondering whether Chiquitita would miss her herd and the life she used to lead. The unanswerable question.

'C'mon, Kirstie!' Lisa called. 'Let's go up to the house, change our clothes and come down for a swim!'

So she tore herself away from the mustang and joined the swimming party, trailing back up to the ranch when the sun was touching the rim of the Basin and sinking fast. By this time, the Jeep parked in the yard told them that Wayne and Walter were home. In fact, Walter had the hood of the car up and was working on a small problem with the engine, cussing as he delved into a toolbox for wrenches that turned out to be the wrong size.

Kirstie, Rob and Lisa passed by quickly, full of news that they wanted to share with Wayne. A quick change into dry clothes was followed by a long, leisurely supper and lots of good, upbeat conversation. By nine-thirty, Lisa and Kirstie were exhausted and crept off to bed.

'Like we did all the hard work – *not!*' Lisa sighed, snuggled up under the sheets.

'Yeah, and we never mentioned the thing between Fresno and Walter to Wayne,' Kirstie added. The incident still troubled her, despite the excitement of the day.

'No, we never did,' Lisa murmured.

'Tomorrow!' Kirstie decided.

'Yeah, tomorrow.'

'G'night . . .'

. . . Silence.

'Ouch!' Wayne held the phone at arm's length and raised his eyebrows. Then gingerly he put it back to his ear while Rob, Kirstie and Lisa ate breakfast next morning.

'Yeah, Mary Ellen, I hear you,' he said patiently. 'But I have a government map here in my office which shows me exactly where the fence line is. And accordin' to the map, the posts are fine . . . No, we haven't crossed on to your land . . . No, the herd isn't gettin' bigger. As a matter of fact, we just held an adoption event in Tamapo a couple of weeks back . . . Yes, Mary Ellen, thanks for callin', and have a nice day!'

'Don't ask!' he warned the kids as he put down the phone. 'She calls herself a spokesperson for all the ranchers north of Squaw Lake. Jeez!'

'At least she didn't show up in person.' Rob reminded his dad to count his blessings, then went to pick up the phone, which was ringing a second time. When he spoke, his face turned serious. 'It's Mom,' he told Wayne. 'There's more news from the hospital.'

Lisa glanced at Kirstie and jerked her head towards the door. 'Better to give them a little privacy,' she said as they stepped out on to the porch.

A pale morning mist still covered the lake and blurred the outline of the distant mountains. It made a welcome change from the scorching sun, so the girls strolled out across the yard, planning to take a peaceful look at Chiquitita in her lakeside enclosure.

'Let's hope it's not bad news,' Kirstie murmured.

'Yeah, poor Rob.'

With their thoughts on the Raburns, Kirstie and Lisa didn't notice at first that they weren't the only visitors to the paddock that morning. They'd reached the fence and were peering through the mist for the black-and-white paint when suddenly Walter's voice broke the silence.

'Come here, Goddam you!'

Lisa and Kirstie whipped around to see the ranch hand riding Prince round the far edge of the enclosure, arm raised, lasso in hand. He went at a lope after Chiquitita, who was obviously trying to stay out of his way. In fact, her ears were laid flat and her tail tucked in – sure signs that she was in full flight mode.

'Uh-oh!' Lisa registered a definite problem. 'Rob isn't gonna like this!'

Walter charged like an old-style cowhand, aiming the lasso and deftly dropping it over the mustang's head. Then he pulled Chiquitita up hard. As the rope tightened, the little mare panicked and tried to flee again.

But Walter simply wound his end of the rope round his saddle horn and made Prince dig in his feet.

The paint's head jerked back and she let out a high-pitched squeal.

'Hey!' Without stopping to think, Kirstie vaulted over the fence and ran towards them. 'What are you doing?'

Walter scowled down at her. 'Butt out!' he warned, his face set in hard lines. Small muscles clicked in his lean jaw and his eyes almost vanished behind a deep frown.

'No!' Kirstie defied him outright. 'I want to know what you think you're doing here!'

'I'm takin' the mare in for freeze brandin',' Walter snapped, dragging so hard on the rope that he brought Chiquitita to her knees. 'Boss's orders.'

'But he didn't mean you to do it like this!' she protested, sick to the stomach, watching the mustang brought down. 'What are you gonna do? Drag her all the way to the barn?'

'If that's what it takes.' Walter was interrupted by a sudden surge of effort from Chiquitita, who managed to stand and turn herself towards the new enemy. She reared up high, dragging Prince off-balance and threatening to unseat his rider. But Walter stayed put, steadying himself by flinging one arm wide and backing Prince up to his original postion.

The combination of a sixteen-hands-high gelding and a tough rider was too much for the little horse. She gasped for breath as the rope tightened again, her eyes rolling and her nostrils wide with fear.

'Stop that!' Kirstie yelled at Walter. 'You're destroying everything that Rob's done with her!'

She ran towards him, but he kicked his foot clear of the stirrup and used the sole of his boot to push her to the ground. 'Since when did I take orders from a stupid, spoiled brat?' he grunted.

Kirstie gasped and crawled clear of Prince's hooves. She could see Chiquitita roll over on to her side, gasping for breath, her body lathered up with sweat.

This was horrible, too awful for words.

'Lisa, go get Wayne!' she cried, turning in desperation towards the fence.

But there was no one there. The girls thought alike – there was only one way to put a stop to this, and Lisa was already sprinting for the house.

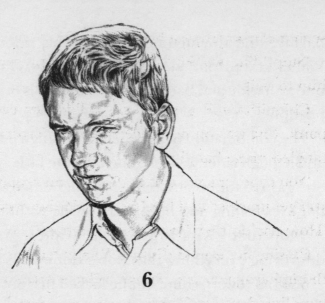

6

Wayne and Rob ran with Lisa down from the house, through the spiky yukka plants and the bright pink cactus flowers. Rob's face was pale with anger and he stumbled in his haste to reach the paddock. He went down on one knee, scrambled up again and sprinted on across the sandy ground.

Walter saw them and knew that he was in deep trouble. He turned on Kirstie. 'See what you did, you stupid kid!'

'Just drop the rope!' she begged.

'You and your interferin' friend are bad news!' he hissed, jerking harder than ever. 'Ain't you ever seen a cowboy rope a horse before?'

'Stop!' She wouldn't argue, she simply wanted him to quit.

Chiquitita still gasped and rolled her eyes in panic. She was on her knees, covered in dirt, her tangled mane hanging over her eyes.

'You rope 'em and if they give you an argument, you get up close and hobble 'em!' Walter insisted. 'How else do they learn who's the boss?'

Closing her eyes in disgust, Kirstie felt her heart thumping against her ribcage. What was this rough handling doing to Chiquitita, she wondered. And just when Rob had worked so brilliantly to build a bond between them.

'Let go of the rope!' Rob yelled now, vaulting the fence and racing towards Walter. Behind him, his dad and Lisa made for the gate and came into the paddock the conventional way.

Stubbornly Walter stuck to his guns. 'My orders are to take the mare up to the barn for freeze markin',' he insisted. 'I've been down here forty-five minutes tryin' to rope the crittur, and I ain't about to let her loose now!'

As Rob spun round to watch Chiquitita sink on to her side, something inside him seemed to snap.

With an angry cry, he threw himself towards Walter, grabbing him around the waist with both arms, intent on dragging him from the saddle.

Walter tried to push him off, but Rob hung on, wrenching with all his strength until the rider lost his balance and slid to the ground.

'Unhitch the rope from the saddle horn!' Rob yelled at Kirstie, still clinging to Walter, who took a close up swing at his opponent and landed a punch to his ribs.

Quickly she unwound the end of the lasso and let it trail to the ground, releasing the pressure on

Chiquitita's neck so that she could stand and breathe again. The horse's first reaction was to run straight at the fence, galloping to within three feet of the rails before deciding not to jump. Instead she slid to a halt, turned, reared and in a frenzy began to race round the edge of the paddock.

Meanwhile, Rob was giving as good as he got in the struggle with Walter. He socked him in the jaw, then launched himself and knocked his opponent off balance again. Walter staggered backwards against Prince, who eyed the fight warily but didn't see the need to move out of the way.

'OK, that's enough!' Wayne ordered, as Walter recovered and threw another punch. He waded in between Rob and Walter, pushing against their chests with his strong arms and prising them apart.

But Rob was beyond taking orders and fought to twist out of his dad's grasp. 'Look what he did to Chiquitita!' he cried, breaking free and plunging towards Wayne's assistant once more. His father caught the back of his shirt as he swung wildly and missed.

'Cool it, Rob!' he muttered. Twisting his fingers

round the neck of Walter's T-shirt, he held him tight until he could make his son listen. 'Take care of the paint. Leave Walter to me.'

So Rob drew in a deep, rasping breath and stepped clear of the fight. Kirstie saw that he was trembling and holding on to his side where he'd taken the first blow. 'C'mon,' she told him, seizing him by the arm and walking him away. 'Between Lisa, you and me, we can talk Chiquitita into a calmer frame of mind.'

'OK, Walter, I'm givin' you a chance to tell me what happened.' Wayne's deep, steady voice pinned his assistant to the spot. 'C'mon, I'm listenin'!'

'Nothin' happened!' came the breathless reply. 'Everythin' was fine before the blonde kid appeared out of the mist and spooked Chiquitita big time. The paint lost it totally. She turned on me and Prince without warnin'. And you know how a mustang acts when she's out of her head. The truth is, I'm lucky to be alive!'

'Hmm.' Wayne grunted. 'I don't buy that, Walter. I figure you were givin' Chiquitita a hard time *before* Kirstie and Lisa showed up.'

'I was doin' my job!' he insisted, sneering nastily.

'And I don't have time to do all this whisperin' stuff. To my mind you spoil a horse's temperament that way. She needs to know you're tougher and stronger than she is – period!'

'Tougher, huh?' Walter's reply had angered Wayne. He'd already let go of Walter's T-shirt, but now he stepped up and pushed him back hard, insulting him and challenging him to retaliate. 'Stronger, huh?'

The assistant tripped over his own feet and landed in the dirt. Roughly Wayne pulled him back up. 'Sure it takes a tough guy to half choke a horse to death. And yeah, you're strong as Superman when you punch a fourteen-year-old kid in the ribs. I saw you do that with my own eyes, Walter, and I thought, "My, that guy is a real hero!" '

'Oh yeah, go ahead and stick up for your own kid!' The humiliation of being pushed around got to Walter. Now he didn't care what he said. He made a flat, chopping motion against his throat. 'I'm sick to here of you and your lousy, spoiled kid. "Walter, do this, Walter drive here, and no, Walter, you can't get a transfer before I say it's OK!" '

'Back off!' Wayne warned. 'You're talkin' yourself out of a job here, boy!'

'Don't call me boy!' Walter was yelling at the top of his voice, his face twisted up in fury. 'And you can take your stinkin' job and do what the heck you like with it! I've had it, OK!'

'Are you quittin'?' Wayne demanded, back in control. He was taller and broader than Walter, who was covered in yellow dust from head to foot.

The question half brought Walter to his senses. He took a sharp breath and began to brush himself down, muttering under his breath but not giving a direct answer.

Wayne measured him up through narrowed eyes. 'Cos if you're not quittin', I'm firin' you,' he said slowly. 'I'll pay what I owe you in wages and then I want you out of Squaw Lake by midday.'

'You can't do that!' Walter argued. 'On what grounds?'

'On account of you bein' cruel to Chiquitita.' Wayne left him in no doubt that he hadn't believed a word of Walter's explanation. 'And on account of the fact that I don't work with a guy who can't follow rules. When I say "No rough methods", I ain't just wastin' my breath. I mean it! On top of which, Walter, I can't say I really took to you from the start!'

The speech left his assistant spluttering with anger, which he then turned on Kirstie and Lisa. 'Look what you did!' he yelled as they quietly kept their distance from the petrified mare. She still raced round the paddock kicking out at the air and shying at shadows.

'This ain't down to the girls,' Wayne stated. He levelled his gaze and stared Walter straight in the eye. 'Ain't no one to blame but you, and you can bet your bottom dollar that's what I'm gonna write in my report to the Bureau. Get this into your thick skull, Walter – I wanna be sure that you take responsibility for this. In fact, if I have anythin' to do with it, I'm gonna see that you never get another job near wild horses as long as you live!'

The incident with Walter Gray caused big distress to Rob's mustang. For well over an hour, while the disgraced assistant stormed off to pack his bags and leave, Chiquitita charged back and forth in the paddock with the crazed intention of escaping all human contact. No way, nowhere, under no circumstances would she risk that rope round her neck again.

Though Rob tried to soothe her and remind her

of the link he'd carefully built up, she would have none of it. And no wonder. There was a burn mark on her neck where Walter had tightened the noose – a visible sign of the violent assault. The inner trauma, however, was even more serious. Whereas twelve hours earlier she'd been alert, curious and warily trusting, when Rob went up to her now she looked like a wild creature under pressure from a deadly enemy. Her ears were back, her teeth bared and the look in her eye told him that she would strike out with her hoof if he came a step nearer.

Kirstie, Lisa and Rob stayed with the horse while Wayne went up to the house to see the disgraced hand off Squaw Lake land.

'Jeez, am I glad your dad got rid of him!' Lisa sighed. 'One look at what he was doing with Chiquitita and I just ran to fetch you. It made me sick to my stomach, and Kirstie too. I can tell you, she took a big risk confronting that guy!'

'Don't tell me!' As they talked, Rob followed Chiquitita's progress round and round the field. He seemed to be waiting for her head to go down – the old sign that she was ready to talk.

Back to square one! Kirstie thought. *Or worse!*

Relief then turned Lisa talkative. 'Honest to goodness, Rob, Kirstie and me had a major problem with Walter. Why, only yesterday we came across him in the barn giving Fresno a hard time. You know the cut on his knee? That was no nail in the wall, believe me!'

'Well, it's over!' Kirstie interrupted. Right now she didn't want to add to Rob's troubles. Up by the house she caught sight of Walter slinging a bag into his old saloon car and stopping to fling some last-minute insults in Wayne's direction.

Rob frowned then nodded. 'I fixed with my mom to fly out to San Francisco this afternoon,' he told them quietly.

'Is your grandpa worse?' Lisa gasped.

'He needs surgery. It's scheduled for Tuesday. Mom wants me to visit tomorrow.'

The facts came across starkly, leaving Lisa and Kirstie silent for a while.

'We'll take good care of Chiquitita for you,' Lisa reminded him.

'She's not doing good,' he sighed. 'It looks to me like she may never get over this.'

As if to emphasise the point, Chiquitita chose this moment to rise on her hind legs and whirl around, looking wildly beyond the fence and neighing shrilly out across Squaw Lake. It was as if she was searching the horizon and calling for her wild herd.

'That's not like you to admit defeat,' Kirstie told Rob quietly.

He glanced at her sharply. 'Who said anything about givin' in?'

She nodded and smiled. 'Just gettin' it straight. If you leave this afternoon, what exactly d'you want us to do with her?'

'You have to start over,' he explained. 'You keep her here by the lake, watchin', waitin'. Then if – *when* – she shows you she wants to parley, you drive her away. It'll be tougher this time, because she has a bad memory of what Walter did. You won't get past the surcingle stage before Tuesday at the earliest.'

'OK.' Looking at Chiquitita's dusty, sweat-stained coat and the raw mark round her neck, Kirstie recognised that she and Lisa had a tough job ahead. In fact, it was hard to think that there was a more unwilling, deep-down mistrustful and wilder horse in the entire world. *Shame on you, Walter Gray!* she said to herself, sensing her stomach twist into anxious knots.

But she wouldn't let Rob know how she felt. She wanted him to leave for the city without worrying over his horse, and so she put on a confident front. 'You wanna bet me ten dollars we've got a stock saddle on her again by the time you get back?'

'No way!' He smiled faintly.

'Twenty dollars if Lisa is riding her round the paddock!'

This time it was Lisa's turn to protest. 'Me?' she cried. 'Are you crazy?'

'OK then. Twenty dollars if *I'm* up in the saddle,' Kirstie persisted. 'C'mon, Rob, I bet I can do it!'

The smile had faded, but he gritted his teeth. 'Twenty dollars!' he agreed, turning with a sigh and walking out of the field.

Lisa and Kirstie watched him for a long time. His shoulders sagged, his head hung low. Then they turned to Chiquitita, who trotted frantically along the fence rail like a caged animal in a zoo. Once in a while she stopped to kick or bite at a post, then with a squeal of frustration she would run on.

'Twenty dollars!' Lisa echoed in a hollow voice.

'Are you saying we can't do it?' Kirstie challenged.

Lisa breathed out noisily. 'Y'know, in my heart I'm not sure I even want to win the bet.'

'How come? What are you saying?'

'I'm figuring that maybe it's better for Chiquitita if we don't,' Lisa admitted. 'I mean, how would it be if we just said OK, we quit?'

'Then what?' Kirstie imagined the disappointment on Rob's face when he returned.

'Then Wayne and Rob both get the picture that the little paint can't ever trust people again. They decide to cut her loose.'

'They send her back to the herd?' For a moment, Kirstie thought about it. Chiquitita out in the desert, free again. A red sunset, a bunch of wild horses galloping across the high plain.

But then she pushed the idea to one side. She called to mind that magic moment when Rob had first reached out to the wild mustang and touched her neck. Boy links up with beautiful creature in a state of perfect harmony. There was meaning in that beyond what went on in everyday life. She wasn't about to let Walter Gray destroy this unique thing.

'Forget it,' she told Lisa briskly. 'Chiquitita will have a wonderful life here.' Gazing at the distressed and traumatised paint horse, Kirstie jutted out her chin. 'Besides, I need that twenty dollars!' she said.

7

Don't touch me! Don't come near me! Chiquitita sent the message loud and clear all through Monday morning.

Kirstie and Lisa saddled Moonpie and Snowbird and rode down to the paddock. But even with them on horseback, Rob's mustang made it plain that she didn't want their company. Still ragged and dirty after the events of the previous day, she kept her distance, snorting and stamping, baring her teeth at them and oozing hostility through every pore of her skin. All the girls could do was to stay outside the fence and sit quietly, knowing that any move on their part would drive Chiquitita into a frenzy.

In the afternoon, Wayne came with them to take a look. He shook his head and frowned. 'Not good,' he muttered. 'But who can blame her? An abused horse is just like an abused kid. There's a big betrayal in there and they feel insecure, afraid, let down. There's no one they can rely on, so they use all their savvy to steer clear of danger.'

'Look at Chiquitita's body language,' Kirstie sighed. 'She's still screaming at us to leave her alone.'

'So what do we do?' Lisa appealed to Wayne.

'Stick around. Wait until she unwinds a little and don't try to force the pace, OK?'

The girls nodded uncertainly. They'd both been hoping for something more precise, but it was clear that Wayne's mind wasn't totally on the subject.

As he went back to the house, they concluded that it must be the problem with Rob's grandpa that was distracting him. In any case, his advice turned out to be accurate – the paint's nerves were still so raw that there was no way they could go into the paddock and work with her.

'Tomorrow!' Kirstie promised after an entire

afternoon of quietly watching. By the following day, the serene setting of the sparkling lake and the mountains sitting far off in a blue heat haze would surely ease Chiquitita's trauma. 'For now, rest and relax. No one's gonna harm you ever again, we promise!'

Early next morning the phone rang in the ranch house kitchen.

Thinking that it would be Rob with news from the hospital, Wayne sprang up to answer it. 'Hi, Wayne Raburn here . . . Oh, yeah, hey there Jeff.'

Lisa gave a small sigh of relief and glanced at Kirstie, who was finishing a glass of orange juice and looking at her watch. Seven thirty – time to go down to the lake and begin work with Chiquitita.

'. . . No, Jeff, I didn't know that. It's the first I heard that Walter lodged a complaint against me. You picked up my email explainin' why I had to let him go? Yeah, that's right, we caught him mistreatin' one of the mustangs. There were four witnessess. So you tell me what the guy can possibly have to complain about.'

Wayne's side of the conversation made Kirstie and Lisa sit up straight.

'That guy has some nerve!' Lisa grumbled. 'Wayne's the one who should be goin' after Walter, not the other way around!'

'He never did look like the type to go quietly,' Kirstie muttered back. 'But don't worry, Wayne will handle it.'

'Sorry, girls.' Their host came off the phone with a deep frown. 'That was my boss, Jeff Oakley. He wants to meet with me in Tamapo at nine o'clock.'

'About Walter?' Kirstie asked. This was just what Wayne didn't need right now. 'Listen, you tell Mr Oakley that Lisa and I saw everything. And if he needs more proof, bring him out here to take a look at Chiquitita's neck!'

Grabbing his hat from the table, Wayne nodded. 'You girls take care,' he ordered. 'I'll be back by midday.'

He'd only been gone ten minutes when a surprise visitor dropped by. Lisa and Kirstie were in the barn, checking the half healed cut on Fresno's knee before saddling Moonpie and Snowbird, when the sound of a light plane landing nearby drew them out into the yard.

The plane had droned overhead, unsettling the saddle horses and no doubt sending Chiquitita into a fresh panic out in the paddock. The pilot had chosen to land on a flat strip of land close to the lake and the girls could already see a figure in a blue denim jacket and matching long, fringed skirt climb out of the small cockpit and stride towards them.

'Mary Ellen Black!' Lisa and Kirstie said as one. Without a shadow of a doubt they were about to face a visit from Wayne's notorious neighbour.

She was tall, with bright auburn hair beneath her white stetson. She walked, head up, shoulders back, glancing haughtily around her, as if the world should pay her attention.

'Uh-oh!' Kirstie muttered.

But Lisa decided to take control of the situation. 'Sorry, Wayne's not here,' she called as the visitor drew near. 'He left for town about fifteen minutes ago!'

The woman didn't even hesitate. 'I'm Mary Ellen Black from Hope Valley. You must be the two kids from Colorado!' Her voice rang out across the yard.

Lisa faltered. How did she know who they were?

'Yeah, that's right. Would you like us to pass on a message?'

'No message!' came the blunt reply. Mary Ellen gestured with her thumb back towards the paddock. 'Was that the mustang that caused all the problems?'

'Er – umm, yeah, that's Chiquitita.' Lisa glanced at Kirstie. Did this woman know everything that went on in the county?

'Chiquitita – precious little one!' Mary Ellen gave a hollow laugh. 'Not so precious, accordin' to Walter Gray!'

OK, that was it! Kirstie felt herself grow irritated with their self-assured visitor. 'What's Walter been saying?' she asked.

Mary Ellen looked her up and down, dismissing her faded jeans and T-shirt, the untidy fair hair scraped back from her face. 'Obviously the paint mare is *loco* – crazy! She's gonna lash out and break someone's neck pretty soon.'

'That's total garbage, and Walter knows it!' Kirstie protested hotly. 'Anyway, how come he's spreading rumours at your place?'

The arch of Mary Ellen's eyebrows warned Kirstie to back off. 'I hired Walter Gray yesterday afternoon as a member of my cutting and roping team. That's why I'm here – to collect his saddle. I believe he quit in a hurry and left it behind by accident.'

'You hired him?' Lisa stumbled over her words. 'But the guy's low life. I wouldn't hire him to clean my boots!'

Mary Ellen withered her with a look. 'Fortunately honey, you're not in any position to hire and fire employees, and I am!' she snapped. 'Now give me the saddle and I can fly out of here. I have a million things to do back home!'

'But you have to listen!' Kirstie barred her way into the barn. 'What Lisa says is true. Walter Gray thinks you can thrash a horse, or cut her or strangle her with a rope to make her mind. His methods belong in the Stone Age, not on a modern ranch!'

Deep frown lines appeared on Mary Ellen's smooth, tanned face. 'Oh yeah, you're the horse whisperer,' she sneered. 'I heard about you! Listen, little girl, when you grow up you'll realise that life ain't a bed of roses, everything nicey-nicey, just speak gently to your horse and she'll love you forever and follow you to the ends of the earth!'

Kirstie scowled back. 'Walter's method sucks!' she insisted. 'He has no patience. If you ask me, he doesn't even like working with animals. He'd be better off working in – in a casino in Vegas, anywhere except on a ranch!'

'As I recall, nobody did ask you, honey.' Without batting an eyelid, Mary Ellen swept by. 'And now if you'll excuse me, I'll pick up that saddle and be on my way!'

'From what I saw, Mary Ellen Black and Walter Gray just about deserve each other!' Kirstie gave her judgement later that morning while she and Lisa were down in the paddock with Chiquitita.

Lisa considered things for a while. 'Nope,' she decided. 'True, Mary Ellen was obnoxious, but not even she deserves Walter!'

Kirstie smiled. They'd been working quietly with the paint for a couple of hours and she was beginning at last to accept their presence in the field. She still kept her distance, but the signals were less hostile. She even gave signs of curiosity and of wanting to join up with Moonpie and Snowbird.

When she did at last come near, nostrils quivering, ears and eyes fixed on them, Kirstie felt a warm glow kindle inside her. This was what they'd waited so patiently for! Yet Wayne and Rob's method demanded that this was the moment when they should push the mustang away again and drive her round the paddock. Next time she approached, and the time after that, she would be more and more determined to join the gang. In the end, Lisa and Kirstie would give in and, having turned the tables completely, they would accept her.

Progress, when it came, was smooth and unforced. Chiquitita definitely wanted to be friends and seemed to be leaving behind her the trauma of Sunday. She came in between the grey and the Appaloosa, breathing noisily and snuffling up to Kirstie's saddle leather as if this was a smell she recognised and held no fear of. Kirstie smiled and stroked the paint's neck, careful to avoid the band of sore, rubbed flesh.

'Good girl!' Lisa whispered. It had been a long two days but at last their patience had paid off. 'What d'you say we try her with the surcingle?' she asked Kirstie.

'Well, if I want to win my twenty dollars, I guess we need to take the next step,' she laughed, but her light-hearted reply disguised a deep nervousness. She was relieved when she saw Wayne's Jeep pull up in the yard. 'This afternoon!' she added quickly.

They left Chiquitita in the paddock and rode up to meet Wayne, who stood waiting for them.

'What's the news from your boss?' Lisa called.

'You really don't want to know!' he replied, taking off his hat and banging off the dust against his leg. 'I'm still tryin' to take in what Jeff told me.'

'That bad, huh?' Kirstie swung out of Moonpie's

saddle and led him into the shade of the barn. 'What's Walter been telling him?'

'First, he claims I had no reason to fire him. He's assured Jeff that he was using an acceptable method of restraint on Chiquitita, and that it was only your over-the-top reaction that sent things spiralling out of control.'

The bare-faced lie stung Kirstie into a hotheaded response. 'Your boss didn't buy that cheap shot, did he? Do you want us to go see him, put him straight?'

'Hold it!' Wayne put up his hand. 'Jeff has to investigate the claim thoroughly and check that the Bureau isn't breaking any employment laws. There's a lot of paperwork, and my boss ain't the prissy, paperwork type. So that's number one reason why he hauled me out to Tamapo.'

'So what's number two?' Lisa asked.

Wearily Wayne ran a hand across his hair before putting his stetson back on. 'This is the real issue, and it wasn't one I was expectin'. From what Jeff told me, Walter is claimin' that I broke the rules by bringin' Chiquitita in off the desert expressly to give her to Rob. He's quoting chapter and verse from the Bureau's own book of herd management, which says that no private ownership of a wild mustang is permissible without going through an official adoption event.'

'But you're the herd manager!' Kirstie pointed out. 'The entire thing is under your control!'

Wayne sighed. 'Walter claims I went over the allocated number. We listed twenty wild horses for adoption earlier this month, and he showed Jeff the record that proves that Chiquitita makes it twenty-one.'

'The sneaky rattlesnake!' Lisa muttered.

Kirstie frowned and thought it through. 'Does that mean Rob might not be able to keep Chiquitita?' The idea hit her like a punch in the ribs.

Wayne gave a non-committal shrug. 'That's worst case scenario, but it could turn out that way, I guess.'

'But that would hit him real hard,' Lisa protested. 'Especially with this stuff about his grandpa. I mean, what would we tell him? Like, Jeez . . . !'

'Well, I haven't had the order to cut her loose yet,' Wayne pointed out. 'Jeff said he needs time to figure it out. He's gonna get back to me pretty soon.'

'I had Walter down as a mean guy, but not this bad!' Kirstie couldn't help thinking about poor Rob. Then of course there was Chiquitita herself. Would she be accepted back into the wild herd now that she'd had contact with civilisation? Or would they shun her and drive her out into the desert, an easy prey for the packs of coyotes and jackals that prowled through the scrub.

'You know he went to work for Mary Ellen Black?' Lisa cut in. She told Wayne about the neighbour's unexpected visit to collect Walter's saddle.

Wayne frowned. 'That's a low move, even for Mary Ellen. I expect she thought it would get under my skin.'

'Yeah, with neighbours like that, who needs enemies?' Lisa sighed.

All three knew they'd reached a low point. *Think about it*, Kirstie told herself. *Right this minute, Rob's grandpa is going through major surgery with only a fifty per cent chance of success. Walter Gray is claiming unfair dismissal against Wayne. And maybe worst of all, Rob might have to lose his beloved little paint mare.*

But there was a stubborn streak in Kirstie which wouldn't let her admit defeat. 'I say we go on

working with Chiquitita, whatever Walter is tryin'
to do,' she declared.

Wayne narrowed his eyes and looked out over
the lake at the mountains. 'Everythin's on a knife's
edge,' he warned. 'We gotta be prepared to lose
her.'

No way! Kirstie thought. *We fight this tooth and
nail!*

Looking for inspiration amongst the beauty of
the landscape, she picked out the dazzling light
on the lake and the shimmering haze that distorted
the tall fingers of rock on the near horizon. Then,
quite by chance, she remembered distant Thunder
Rock, the sacred site of old. Somehow it gave her
strength to remember that young warriors had
fasted alone and sought visions there.

And Squaw Lake itself attracted birds and
animals over great distances. She could make out
an eagle wheeling across the blue sky, a few deer
skipping and jumping across the rocky ground.
Then, nearer and more distinct, she picked out
the herd of wild horses standing on the flat rim of
rock that overlooked the lake.

Too many to count, but approaching two
hundred in number, the mustangs gazed down into

the basin where Chiquitita grazed in the paddock. Greys, sorrels, paints and Appaloosas peacefully surveyed her new home, and it struck Kirstie that they were giving the Raburns' spread their blessing.

'Yes!' she breathed. 'The little one is doing OK again. She's safe. There's no need to worry!'

8

Kirstie's positive thinking carried through to the next day. At breakfast she told Wayne that the plan was to work with Chiquitita as if there was no threat hanging over their heads.

'Lisa and I will keep out of your hair, so you do what you have to do as if we're not here.'

Wayne said he was grateful. 'Jeff Oakley wants another meeting in town later today. I guess I gotta bite the bullet and hear what he has to say.'

'Will he decide what to do with Chiquitita?' Lisa asked anxiously.

'Yeah. But I'm not gonna give her up without a

fight,' Wayne assured them. When the phone rang, he jumped, then steadied himself by grabbing the edge of the table. 'That'll be Rob from the hospital.'

This was the first news about Rob's grandfather since the surgery, so Lisa and Kirstie gathered around the phone as Wayne answered the call. They watched his face, saw him nod his head. 'Triple by-pass,' he murmured. 'Eight hours? Yeah, OK, son. You tell your grandpa from me to hang on in there.'

The short conversation ended with a click of the phone, then Wayne looked at the girls. 'He made it through the surgery OK. They have him in the high-dependency coronary unit, and it'll be twenty-four hours before he's off the critical list.'

'But so far, so good,' Lisa breathed.

'How did Rob sound?' Kirstie asked.

'Tired,' Wayne admitted. 'They were awake all night, sittin' by the bed. And Rob would want to take care of his mom and grandma too. He's a good kid in that way.'

Lisa and Kirstie quietly agreed.

'Listen, Wayne,' Kirstie went on. 'I've been figuring out this problem Walter's given us over

108

keeping Chiquitita. Is it the fact that you didn't take her to an adoption event that's the issue, or is it that you've taken one extra mare from the wild herd, which brings their number down too low?'

'A little of each, I guess.'

'OK, so as herd manager, you can convince your boss that you have the space and the expertise to school a mustang, and that to send her back now might be dangerous for her. Maybe the herd won't accept her back – she's a wild animal who's grown used to human contact, and that's never good. She has the smell and feel of domesticity about her now.'

'You mean the wild herd might kick her out if we try to send her back?' Lisa asked.

'Yeah. They were out there last night, watching her settle into her new home. I reckon they've accepted that this is where she is.' As Kirstie talked on, she grew more sure that Wayne had a good case to put before Jeff Oakley. 'And that stuff about reducing the size of the wild herd, why don't you promise Jeff that you'll balance the numbers next time you do an adoption event?'

'Huh!' Wayne nodded enthusiastically. 'Good thinkin'. We hold our next event in the fall. Twenty more horses are due to come off the range, so we just pull out nineteen instead. That'd work!'

Lisa gave Kirstie a hopeful grin. 'How d'you get along with your boss?' she asked Wayne.'

'Jeff's as stubborn as an old mule,' he muttered. 'But we get along fine.'

'So, as far as the firing Walter issue goes, he'll eventually take your word that you had your reasons,' Lisa assured him.

'Yeah, but if Jeff takes my side, what's that gonna do to Walter's frame of mind?' Wayne wondered. 'He's out to get me, and if he can't do it legally, it's gonna make him totally flip. That's when we really got ourselves a problem.'

'Well, let's worry about that later,' Kirstie said, taking her hat from the hook and setting out for the barn. 'Top of our list is to make sure Chiquitita is still here when Rob gets back from San Francisco!'

You have to be focused. You have to fix your mind on earning Chiquitita's trust and block out every other thought! Kirstie told herself. *If they can put a man on the moon, I can join up with a wild horse!*

She'd worked hard in the paddock all morning.

With Lisa and Snowbird standing by, she'd ridden Moonpie and managed the surcingle and the saddle blanket but hadn't progressed as far as the actual saddle.

By midday, Lisa had admitted to being beaten by the sun. 'I need some shade and a cool drink from the icebox,' she'd told Kirstie. 'D'you want me to bring one down for you?'

'Yeah, I'm gonna try her one more time with the saddle while you're gone.'

So Lisa had ridden away from the lake, leaving Kirstie and Moonpie alone in the paddock with Chiquitita.

The paint stood at a distance, taking in the new one-on-one situation. She looked beautiful in the dazzling light, the white patches of her coat standing out, the dark ones gleaming. Already the rope burn round her neck was fading. She seemed content for Kirstie to dismount and take up the spare saddle from the fence rail, as if prepared at last to let go of the bad memories created by Walter Gray.

Maybe this time! Kirstie told herself, talking gently to Chiquitita as she approached. The heavy saddle pulled at the muscles in her arms and the stirrups

111

clunked against her legs as she walked. 'Nice'n easy!' she breathed, giving the paint a long time to sniff at the stock saddle. 'You've done this once before with Rob, remember? And Moonpie and Snowbird do it every day of their lives, no problem!'

Chiquitita turned her head to follow Kirstie's smooth movements. She flinched at the first touch of the saddle on her back, but then she relaxed. *Oh yeah, I recall this! Smells kinda weird, feels strange, but it doesn't bite!*

Kirstie patted her and reached under her belly for the cinch strap. She watched out warily for a swift kick but none came. 'You're a good girl,' she soothed, slipping the strap through its buckle and tightening it. She had to tell herself not to hurry, to act like she had all day.

So she stepped away and let Chiquitita walk freely. The mare gave an experimental shake of her whole body and seemed surprised to find the saddle still on her back at the end of it. She tried a small buck – same thing. So she trotted, loped and came back to a walk. Nope, no way was she gonna lose this thing on her back. So what? It wasn't doing any harm.

Kirstie found herself smiling at the way the mare adjusted to the experience. Feeling confident, she moseyed across and gave a couple of pulls at the horn and stirrups, plus a friendly slap at Chiquitita's rump. 'You ready to take my weight here?' she murmured.

As if understanding the question, the paint braced herself and stood perfectly still.

'Easy!' Kirstie breathed, daring to raise her left foot and slide it into the stirrup.

Chiquitita jumped sideways and kicked backwards with her front leg.

Kirstie released her foot in time to keep her balance. 'Not sure, huh?' she whispered.

To her surprise, it was Chiquitita who came back of her own accord, snuggling up alongside Kirstie and inviting rubs and pats. Kirstie obliged with a grin. 'Yeah, you're real sorry now for spooking when there was no need. Are you gonna let me try again? Good girl!'

The second time she slid her foot into the stirrup, the obliging little mustang held steady and allowed her to swing her leg over the saddle. Now Kirstie had achieved as much as Rob had at the weekend.

'Wow!' She felt her heart swell with pride that she, Kirstie Scott, had been accepted by the wild horse. *This is a high point of my life!* she told herself, breathing deeply and holding her head up. Touched to the core, she took a moment to say thank you to the magnificent, spirited creature whose trust she had gained.

Then the precious bubble was burst by the hasty reappearance of Lisa, who came riding down from the house. Something urgent had happened, Kirstie could tell, so she slid smoothly from the saddle and quickly unbuckled the cinch, lifting the tack off and swinging it over the fence rail before Lisa reached the paddock.

Meanwhile, Chiquitita took refuge from the emergency at the far side of the paddock.

'Kirstie, listen up!' Lisa exclaimed, reining Snowbird to a sliding stop. 'I just took a phone call from Mary Ellen Black!'

'Isn't Wayne home yet?' she asked. He always seemed to be out when his neighbour called or dropped by.

'No, he's still in town seein' Jeff Oakley. So I had to talk to Mary Ellen, and guess what, she's warnin' us to watch out for Walter Gray!'

The name made the small hairs at the back of Kirstie's neck stand up. 'Why, what did he do now?'

'Jeez, you're not gonna believe this. Mary Ellen said it took her less than twenty-four hours to work out what kind of a guy he was and be sorry she ever hired him!' Lisa slid breathlessly to the ground and held tight to her Appaloosa's reins.

'C'mon, tell me what happened!' Kirstie urged. 'Did he start beating up on her horses?'

Lisa shook her head. 'Last night he went totally off the rails, drinkin' and bustin' stuff in the barn. She said he was yellin' like a crazy man, swearin' he would get even with Wayne. None of Mary Ellen's guys could talk any sense into him.'

'Huh!' In a way, Kirstie wasn't sorry. This kind of behaviour wouldn't win Walter any friends and it would make it easier for Wayne to convince the Bureau people that he'd been right to fire the guy. 'Is that it?'

Again Lisa had to pause to take a deep breath. 'Nope,' she went on. 'Mary Ellen told her hands to let Walter sleep off his drink in the bunkhouse overnight, then this mornin' they had orders to kick him off Hope Valley territory. And this is where it gets real interesting! Walter gave them a fight. Lots more furniture got broken. Then he headed out for the runway where Mary Ellen keeps her two-seater Cessna. And what does he do? He climbs in the cockpit and turns on the engine, leaves the guys standing on the tarmac with their jaws hangin' open, watchin' him take off!'

Kirstie's eyes widened in surprise. 'Does he even know *how* to fly a plane?'

Lisa shrugged. 'I didn't get a chance to ask. This only happened less than an hour ago. Mary Ellen called the Tamapo sheriff, then she tried to call Wayne. The phone's been ringin' in the empty house for the last half hour.'

'Why? What was so important?' Kirstie frowned. 'Was it something Walter said?'

A nod this time showed that her hunch had been right.

'Did he threaten Wayne?' she guessed again.

'You got it! Last night he swore he'd get even if it was the last thing he did. And listen, Kirstie, it wasn't just Wayne he was threatenin'. It was you and me both!'

'That figures!' Kirstie groaned.

'*And!*' Lisa hadn't finished yet. 'The guy's nuts.

He was yellin' that he wouldn't rest until he'd dealt with the horse that had caused all the problems in the first place!'

'Chiquitita? That's totally crazy!' Kirstie felt her heart thud and then set off at a rapid rate. Illogical though it was, she had no doubt that anger combined with alcohol could push Walter into a senseless act of bitter revenge. 'What are we gonna do?'

Lisa shook her head. 'I was hopin' you would tell me. I just took the call and freaked out. I mean, the guy's got a sore head and a heap of anger inside him. He's in a plane he probably can't even fly properly, and the last Mary Ellen's ranch hands saw of him he was headin' this way!'

A band seemed to tighten round Kirstie's rapidly beating heart. Instinctively she glanced up into the blue sky, then at the three horses – Moonpie and Snowbird, fully tacked up and standing alert by the gate, Chiquitita growing restless by the fence closest to the lake.

'I figure we should get Chiquitita under cover before Walter gets here!' she gasped, forgetting the basic rule about working with horses in her sudden panic. Instead of looking like she had all the time in the world, she set off at a run across the paddock.

The sudden move sent Chiquitita into flight mode. She plunged into a lope to avoid Kirstie, tossing her head and laying her ears flat against her head.

It was Lisa who first realised that it wasn't only Kirstie's panic that had sent the horse careering off like this. She noticed that Snowbird and Moonpie were also spooked. They danced and skittered around, heads up, ears pricked, listening to a faint droning sound in the sky.

Plane! Not visible yet, but definitely coming closer. She looked up to the west, beyond Squaw Lake, and picked out a tiny silver dot in the blue expanse. The sun dazzled her. For a second she hoped she was wrong, but then she shaded her eyes and took a second look. Yeah, a tiny two-seater with twin propellors, heading their way.

'Look out, Kirstie. Here he comes!' There was no time now to wait for Chiquitita to settle down and come quietly up to the barn. The truth was they were stranded in the open with the two saddle horses and the mustang.

Kirstie heard the plane and stood helplessly in

the middle of the paddock. 'Maybe it's not Walter. It could be anybody!' she insisted.

But the plane was losing height, heading directly for Squaw Lake.

Lisa shook her head. 'It's him,' she said flatly.

As the pilot brought the plane low overhead, Chiquitita grew terrified. The droning, whining noise of the engine seemed to fill her head and send her crazy, so that she flew around the paddock, rearing and bucking, raising a cloud of dust.

'Back off!' Kirstie waved both arms at the plane, begging Walter to leave them alone.

But he banked the plane and began to circle overhead, flying lower still so that he almost clipped the top of a stand of pine trees at the far side of the lake. Quickly he regained height, then turned around, coming back across the water so low that Lisa and Kirstie could see the shape of the pilot in the cockpit and the round blur of the propellors.

'Jeez!' Lisa gasped, ducking and covering her head.

Kirstie gritted her teeth and stood fast. The back draught from the Cessna practically knocked her over as Walter swooped down on the paddock.

The three horses went wild. Moonpie and Snowbird reared up, while Chiquitita changed course to charge across the centre of the paddock, aiming straight for the high fence. She stopped a foot short, wheeled around and zigzagged here and there, desperate to find a way out.

And the plane was already banking and turning again, heading back for a third time.

'This is his stupid idea of revenge!' Lisa groaned.

Kirstie licked her dry lips. *Thud-thud* – her heart pummelled against her ribs. She doubted that Chiquitita could take another swoop. The horse was sweated up and frothing at the mouth, in a total frenzy.

But Walter had no intention of letting up. He flew over low and fast, with a terrifying roar and a rush of warm wind.

Chiquitita squealed and reared. She set off at a gallop towards the fence, already knowing that she couldn't clear it, determined this time to use her weight and speed to crash straight through.

'She'll kill herself!' Lisa yelled.

Kirstie watched in horror as the plane passed so low that the tip of its wing almost dipped into the water as Walter banked and turned it around.

The paint charged the fence and threw herself at the rails. She ploughed through, splintering the wood and scattering the poles. One deep stumble in amongst the thorn bushes and she was back up, galloping on across the desert.

Free again.

9

Kirstie and Lisa watched Chiquitita race across the Basin. They saw the plane turn around and start to pursue her.

'Why won't he quit?' Kirstie cried, afraid that Walter Gray would drive the mustang beyond her limit into some suicidally dangerous act.

Lisa was too angry to answer. Instead, she ran to Snowbird and jumped into the saddle, grabbing Moonpie's reins and leading him across to Kirstie. 'Get on!' she yelled.

Her voice broke Kirstie free of the nightmare. She did as Lisa told her, and soon their horses were on Chiquitita's trail, heading down the side of Squaw Lake and up into a narrow barranca which led on to the flat plains to the north west.

Still Walter brought the plane down low and tormented the little paint. As the engine whined overhead she would rear and stagger backwards, then plunge to the ground in terror, sometimes falling on to her knees and struggling to regain her balance. This gave Lisa and Kirstie time to narrow the gap, but always she was up again and galloping on before they could reach her.

The cruel game went on relentlessly in the midday heat. The empty desert was a huge playground for the psycho behind the controls of the plane. Intent on revenge, he buzzed Chiquitita from left and right, always dipping to a dangerous ground-skimming level, threatening to smash into the horse, but rising at the last second and turning around to try again.

Kirstie found herself struggling to breathe. Each time the plane dived, she choked with fear for the poor mustang. Her heart would stop, then hammer again against her ribs as she drove Moonpie on at a crazy, strength-draining pace.

'That little paint is gonna drop dead out of sheer

terror!' Lisa warned, leaning low over Snowbird's neck and galloping on.

Walter had just buzzed them again and changed Chiquitita's course. Now she was heading directly for Great Bird Lake and the tall rock face where the cave dwellings were. Her pace was dropping a little and her head had begun to hang out of sheer exhaustion.

'Pray that he runs out of fuel soon!' Kirstie muttered. It seemed the only reason why Gray would let up on them. And there was no help around – no horse riders with radios to call for reinforcements, no Jeep drivers exploring the deserted Zuni site – just vast, empty desert.

By the time Chiquitita reached Great Bird Lake, she was stumbling and on the point of collapse. Snowbird and Moonpie were also worn out, dark with sweat, with white lather across their withers and under their bellies.

Even now, Gray kept on the pressure, flying dangerously close to the caves, then wheeling suddenly like a clumsy metal bird and rising clear of the cliff. Chiquitita meanwhile sought shelter by Water Cave, unable to take another step.

'That's a good move!' Kirstie whispered, relaxing

slightly when she saw what the paint had done. 'Even crazy Walter Gray won't fly too close to the rocks!'

Seeing that Chiquitita had come to a standstill, Kirstie and Lisa eased up at a respectful distance, waiting close by the water's edge for Gray to quit. After he'd gone, they would begin over again with the mustang, gentling her and persuading her back to Squaw Lake in time for Rob's return.

But Kirstie had been forgetting that Gray was totally out of his bitter, twisted mind. In fact, he was enjoying this game of torture way too much to pack up and go home. So he turned the plane around one more time and came in from behind the cliff.

The girls couldn't see him, but they heard the engine's approach and stared fearfully into the sky. The intense midday sun made the Zuni dwellings flicker behind a glaring heat haze. Nothing seemed solid or real as yet again the tormenting plane approached.

In the shade of Water Cave, Chiquitita sagged wearily. She was close against the overhanging entrance, a little below the primitive drawings etched into the foot of the cliff. The one that stood out from the shadows startled Kirstie into giving a small cry.

'What is it?' Lisa reined Snowbird around.

Kirstie drew breath. 'Nothing. It was the eyes carved in the rock. They spooked me.'

The evil eyes of the Water Baby herself, turned to stone by the Zuni shaman, watching everyone who passed by.

Just then, Walter Gray roared his aircraft into sight. He was directly overhead, dipping low, screaming his engine.

Chiquitita heard, but all her energy was burned up. Defeated, she sank to the ground.

The plane dropped steeply – too sharply – towards the shore. As it plummeted, Lisa and Kirstie heard the engine half-stall then choke back into life. But the split-second emergency made Walter lose more height. The tip of one wing clipped the side of the cliff and threw him off-balance, the other wing tilting and skimming the yellow sand.

Kirstie put her hands to her face. Lisa gave an agonised shout.

The plane was out of control. One wing dragged along the shore. The tip snapped off, swinging

the whole machine towards the water. They saw Walter try to regain height, but like a bird with a broken wing, it failed to take off. Instead it plummeted belly first into the lake, raising huge spray, then slowing until at last the engine cut out and the whole thing stopped.

There was a stunned silence. Kirstie could see the two propellors churn through the water then grind to a halt. Though both wings were battered and broken, the body of the plane seemed mainly intact and floating for the time being in about ten feet of water.

Now Kirstie and Lisa were torn. Their hearts still went out to poor, tortured Chiquitita, lying exhausted by the entrance to the cave. But there was a guy in the plane who was making no attempt to climb out of the cockpit before it sank.

'What happened? Did he knock himself out?' Lisa whispered in the weird silence.

'Or worse?' Kirstie knew that the force of the crash could've killed Gray. She watched the broken plane bob in the clear water and a thin film of rainbow-coloured oil spread across the surface.

'We need to concentrate on Chiquitita!' Lisa hissed, pointing to the spot by the cave where the mare was struggling back to her feet.

'And leave the guy to drown?' Kirstie's voice was faint. 'We can't do that, can we?'

There was deep doubt in Lisa's eyes. 'He's a horse-torturer. It's all he deserves,' she protested.

'I know it . . .' Kirstie felt herself being ripped apart.

'. . . But?' Lisa added.

'But we can't let him die, whatever he did to Chiquitita.'

That was it – the bottom line. A man could be dying and they had in all conscience to prevent it.

In any case, the mustang was no longer in immediate danger. They could pull Gray out of the plane and return to help her, though what they'd do with him after they'd rescued him, they had no idea. This wasn't in their minds as they dismounted and left Moonpie and Snowbird on the shore. They simply waded into the water on their grim mission to save the person that right that moment they hated most in the entire world.

At first, Kirstie felt the flat stones on the bed of the lake slide and scrape under her feet. But soon she was waist deep and Lisa had already launched herself into a strong breast-stroke. So she too took the full plunge, striking out towards the wreck, which seemed to be settling lower into the water.

What would they do if it had sunk out of sight by the time they arrived? She pictured the top of the cockpit disappearing below the surface, and with it their only realistic chance of pulling Gray out alive. The idea made her put more energy into her swimming – the last thing she wanted was to be left feeling guilty over not having tried hard enough to rescue him.

That was a harsh thought, she knew, but it was true that deep down she felt no scrap of pity for Walter Gray.

There was twenty yards now between her and the crashed plane and it really was settling deep into the water. Kirstie kicked hard and surged across the distance, drawing level with Lisa and gasping out a question. 'How do we get into the cockpit?'

'We have to find the door. Does it open at the side, or on top?'

'At the side,' Kirstie guessed.

They were swimming now through the thin film of oil that surrounded the sinking plane and were almost able to reach out and touch the nearest wing. As yet, though, they couldn't see into the cockpit.

What if he's dead already? Kirstie thought. *All there is in there is a corpse. What then?* She glanced back to the shore to see Chiquitita already regaining her strength, treading nervously by the water's edge and keeping her distance from Snowbird and Moonpie. The tiers of cave dwellings towered behind the three horses like a golden honeycomb.

'I can see him!' Lisa yelled. She'd swum round to the far side and used the tilt of the plane in the water to peer into the cockpit. 'He's movin'! Oh, Jeez, Kirstie, his face is covered in blood!'

'Hold on. Is there a door there?' Turning on to her side, Kirstie swam around the nose of the plane to join her friend. As she looked at the cockpit from the fresh angle, Gray's face suddenly appeared behind the glass.

His hair was plastered to his thin face, his cheek bleeding badly. But worst of all, his expression was twisted into wild terror. Already up to his chest in water, he saw them and began to bang at the pane.

'Where's the handle?' Kirstie gasped, swallowing water as she lunged for the door.

The sudden movement tilted the plane even

further on to its side. Now water lapped against the window and they could see Walter yell and hammer again, even more urgently than before.

At last, by feeling below the water line, Kirstie's fingers made contact with the handle. She turned it and began to pull, but nothing happened. 'I can't open it!' she gasped. 'Lisa, you try!'

A few more moments passed before Lisa came up with the same result. 'I guess it's pressure of water on the outside,' she reported.

Inside the cockpit, the level had risen to the trapped man's neck. He pressed his face against the pane and scrabbled the smooth surface with his fingertips.

'We have to break the glass!' Kirstie decided, watching in horror as the red stain of Walter's blood dribbled down.

'What with? I know!' Lisa's first thought was to dive to the bottom and bring up a stone heavy enough to smash a hole in the cockpit.

Kirstie was about to do the same when she spotted a metal bar hanging loose from the broken wing. Maybe she could pull at that and lever it clear? It would make the perfect tool for shattering glass.

She swam clumsily, dimly aware of a faint yell from Walter inside the plane. He must have thought they were abandoning him, because the yell rose to a scream. Ignoring him, Kirstie reached the broken wing strut and pulled with all her strength.

By this time, Lisa had reappeared. But her stone was small and the cockpit's glass was reinforced. It needed Kirstie's metal bar. She found a place under the wing where she could brace herself and tug even harder. This time, the bar pulled clean away from the thin steel skin.

Kirstie lurched back, clutching it in both hands. Then, fast as she could, she rejoined Lisa. 'Swim clear!' she yelled, treading water and wielding the bar like a truncheon. But she found she could get no force into her blows from her position in the water.

'I'm gonna climb on top!' she cried, asking Lisa to hoist her on to the wing, where she knelt only inches away from Gray's desperate face. Showing him the bar so that he could protect himself from the splinters of glass, she swung it sideways then crashed it against the window with all her force.

The bar met the safety glass with a dull crunch.

Kirstie saw the window craze over in a thousand tiny fragments, but it was still intact. A second blow stove the whole thing in. There was a space where the window used to be.

Now the water poured through the gap, bringing Gray's head up against the cockpit roof. He thrust his hand sideways through the smashed window for Kirstie to catch hold of. She grabbed the skinny wrist, felt the fingers grasp hers, yelled to Lisa for help. 'Let's pull him out before it goes under!'

Then Lisa was there with her, ducking under the water to grab Walter's shirt and tug him clear of his seat. She found one of his legs was jammed under the control panel and had to resurface for air. One gulp and she was under again, bending and twisting the trapped leg until it was free then rising to help Kirstie make the final effort to pull him out of the wreck.

'OK, we're gonna do it!' Kirstie told Walter. 'We're getting you out before it goes down!'

But only just. As they hooked their arms under him and dragged him clear, a surge of air bubbles escaped from the undercarriage. It was like a dying breath for the plane, because as the air escaped, the wings which had been acting as floats disappeared under the water. Within seconds, the whole machine had sunk to the bottom.

Walter clung to Kirstie and Lisa. 'Can't swim!' he gasped, his face ghastly white now that the water had washed the blood away. 'My leg's busted!'

'Quit thrashin' around!' Lisa ordered. She and Kirstie began to drag him towards the shore – an easy job between the two of them, but made more difficult by Gray's terrified writhing in the water.

Now who's the main man? Kirstie thought. *This guy needs a bottle of whisky and a whole plane to make him feel big and powerful. But really he's just a wimp!*

Still, they had to make sure he was safe. They got him to dry land and let him drop on to the pebbles, where he gasped and coughed the water out of his lungs. He yelled angrily when Kirstie rolled him on to his side into the recovery position. 'I told you, my leg's busted!'

'So can you breathe OK on your back?' she asked. Blood was beginning to pour from the gash in his cheek again, so she glanced up towards Moonpie and Snowbird, whose small saddle-bags might contain something to mop up the mess.

The two saddle horses stood patiently in the sun,

waiting to be called on. But where had Chiquitita got to?

The last time Kirstie had looked, the mustang had been gathering herself together after the nightmare chase, keeping separate from the trained horses and still seeking shade. But now there was no sign of her on the shore. Or under the towering cliff, or by the dark entrance to the Water Cave.

Kirstie got to her feet and looked again. The blue water lapped against the pebbles but the ancient cave dwellings were silent in the heat. The Water Cave yawned open behind its untidy heap of boulders. A pair of carved, staring eyes watched the scene, giving nothing away.

'Chiquitita!' Kirstie whispered.

A breeze lifted from the lake and drifted across the shore, on up the hill to the cave. It sighed through the thin aspens at the foot of the cliff, shaking their silver-green leaves, then rose through the caves like a host of whispering voices. 'Where are you, precious one?' they murmured. 'Don't go, little girl. Come back!'

10

Kirstie felt empty inside. She and Lisa had chosen to save Walter Gray's life, but they'd lost Rob's beautiful mustang.

The desert and high plains were vast open spaces where a horse could run forever and never be caught. Chiquitita was out there, free but alone and vulnerable, an easy prey for animals with sharp teeth and claws.

'Kirstie, we need to get Walter back to Squaw Lake!' Lisa's voice broke through.

She shook herself. She looked down at the injured man and saw that he was in pain. 'Can you get on a horse and ride?' she asked him.

Still coughing, and with blood streaming down his face and staining his wet shirt bright red, Gray raised the upper half of his body and propped himself on his elbows. 'You'll have to lift me on,' he grunted. 'After that, I reckon I can make it.'

Kirstie glanced at Lisa. 'Let's put him on Moonpie. You ride Snowbird and dally them back.'

'What about you?' Lisa shrank from the role of leading Walter on the long, slow trek back to the Raburns' spread.

'I'm staying,' Kirstie answered firmly.

'Alone? On foot?' Now Lisa was even less happy about the solution. The sun was scorching hot; Kirstie was just one girl against a vast, hostile environment.

But Kirstie was determined. 'Chiquitita may still be around here somewhere. I'm gonna track her down.'

Lisa shook her head and sighed. 'This is needle in a haystack stuff, you realise.'

'Maybe, but I have to try.'

'OK.' Lisa gave in. She turned back to Walter and offered to help raise him to his feet.

Groaning with pain, he hitched his arm round

her shoulder, took his weight on one leg and allowed her to pull him upright. 'Watch the leg!' he warned roughly.

Meanwhile, Kirstie went to fetch Moonpie. She walked him to the water's edge and waited for Walter to hop and hobble towards them.

'Bring him into the lake,' Lisa said. 'It's gonna be easier to haul Walter into the saddle if we can get the water to take some of his weight.'

So Kirstie waded in with the tall grey, who stood obediently up to his belly while the girls positioned the injured man then lifted him sideways out of the water into the saddle.

'Can you lean back and ease one leg over?' Lisa asked him, wading round to the far side.

'No way!' he grunted.

'Then you'll have to sit side-saddle and hang on to the horn.'

Nodding, he roughly told Kirstie to lead Moonpie back to the shore. 'Let's move it,' he muttered, gritting his teeth as Moonpie's movement disturbed his broken leg.

Slumped sideways in the saddle, Gray cut a pathetic picture as Lisa ran for Snowbird. Kirstie knew she should feel sorry that the man was in pain, but she was too angry at what he'd done. 'Find Wayne and tell him exactly what happened, OK!' she said to Lisa, handing over Moonpie's reins. 'Get him to send people out to help search for Chiquitita. We need to locate her before nightfall.'

'Sure thing,' Lisa replied anxiously, still reluctant to leave Kirstie alone. 'You take care, you hear!'

Kirstie nodded, glancing up at the cliff beyond the cave. 'Maybe she's resting some place in the shade.'

'Yeah, along with a hundred rattlesnakes!' Lisa muttered. She looked her friend in the eye. 'I mean it, Kirstie, don't take risks, OK!'

Kirstie's promise sent Lisa and Walter Gray on their way along the lake shore. They plodded steadily east, leaving Kirstie to search for the missing paint.

In spite of the turmoil of her emotions, Kirstie settled to the task of tracking Chiquitita. She needed to find a set of prints minus iron shoes and to follow them, wherever they led. This wasn't so easy on the scuffed, sandy surface around Water Cave. Too much activity had blurred the prints and the earth was too soft to hold the shapes.

Disappointed, Kirstie glanced up at the carvings on the nearby rock. The man on the horse, the deer and other shapes were comforting reminders that people had once lived here, but the staring eyes belonging to the monster who had inhabited the cave made her shiver. Though they were carved into the rock, they seemed to follow her wherever she went. She trod slowly along the water's edge, still searching for the right set of prints, looked back and found they were still staring at her.

Perhaps the old tribes had been right, and there was an evil spirit still inhabiting this place. Maybe the force had allowed Walter Gray to torture the wild horse and let him escape serious injury in the crash.

No, forget it! Sternly Kirstie dismissed the superstition and went on searching until she came across Chiquitita's tracks. The first clear set pointed up the slope towards the ancient Zuni caves, where the earth was less sandy and the prints became clearer.

So the paint had left the shore and headed for shelter from the heat. The wise move would have given her time to regain her strength before taking flight across open country.

'Pray she's still here!' Kirstie murmured as she followed the tracks. They led straight up through the aspens and under the overhang of the tall cliff face.

Here the surface of the ground was rocky and unluckily for Kirstie the trail ended.

She crouched low and stared hard into the shadows, looking for droppings, strands of horse hair caught on a bush, or any other sign that Chiquitita had rested up under the ledge. She drew a blank.

Stepping backwards into the glare of the sun, Kirstie heard a low rustle of dry aspen leaves, which had collected in the angle of rock at the base of the cliff. She stiffened. Snake! No doubt about it. But how big, and what kind? If the rustle developed into a rattle, then she knew she was in deep trouble.

She held her breath, telling herself not to run. Any sudden movement would alarm the snake.

Slowly it showed its flat head. Its forked tongue flickered in and out; its yellow eyes stared.

Not a rattler, but a nondescript dark-brown snake which Kirstie didn't recognise. She relaxed a little, watching three or four feet of scaly reptile emerge from the dead leaves. It slithered across the rock into the sun, raised its head and looked at her again.

Kirstie froze. Rattler or not, it could still have a dangerous bite. The eyes mesmerised her, reminding her of the eyes on the rock.

Soon though, the snake seemed to lose interest. Preferring the shade to the glare of the sun, he slid sideways and disappeared back under the ledge.

Breathing again, Kirstie reminded herself to take more heed of Lisa's warning not to take risks. Having lost Chiquitita's trail, she figured she had better climb the remainder of the slope to the bottom tier of cave dwellings and take a look there. After all, there was only up or down, so it was a fifty-fifty bet that the horse had continued on.

She soon reached the square entrance to the nearest cave. She peered inside the dark, dusty space and immediately knew that Chiquitita would never have taken refuge there. The room was small and cell-like – exactly the kind of place that a wild horse would shun. It was too easy to be trapped inside, too cut off from the natural signals that would warn her of approaching danger.

Kirstie sighed and stood back. Peering up at the cliff face and its hundred square openings, she did take time to wonder what life here had been like centuries ago. The honeycomb rock would have been a natural choice for the old tribes. The caves and tunnels were dry and cool, and the high levels gave a good lookout over the lake. She imagined fires to ward off cold in the winter, Zuni women cooking cornbread over glowing cinders, the men gathering to tell tales and sing songs in the quiet evenings.

Now, however, there were only tiny echoes remaining – the crumbling doorways, the small windows carved into the rock and the faint drawings smoothed out by the wind. Visitors seldom came here to see and search for the past. The place was sad and lonely.

Shaking herself out of the mood which the cave dwellings had brought on, Kirstie chose not to climb the worn rock steps to the next level. Instead, she went down through the trees to the shore, gazing out across the lake for a moment, then turning to the Water Cave. She looked hard at the high, arched entrance which was largely hidden behind the stack of boulders, supposedly dumped there by the wicked spirit to keep out intruders.

But there must be a way in, Kirstie thought to herself, finding that, almost despite herself, she was drawn to the mysterious, narrow opening. She felt her skin prickle as she came near, but told herself to forget the superstitions and carry on. After all, there was a slim chance that Chiquitita had chosen the cave as a refuge.

Her feet crunched over the loose stones. So much for catching the mustang unawares! If she was in the cave, she would be fully alert, ready to run again. Kirstie frowned and walked on. Just one look to satisfy herself . . .

She paused. There was a definite presence around.

The Water Baby? The demon who snatched babies. The destroyer.

No. This was something alive and breathing, a powerful creature standing behind the boulders.

Kirstie's heart missed a beat. How had she detected the living presence? She couldn't hear a thing, there was no solid evidence, yet she knew.

But what to do next? Was the creature friend or foe? Did she dare risk taking the few steps to find out?

In the end, she didn't have to.

Something stirred. Unseen hooves clattered over the stones and the horse appeared.

He was tall and magnificent. He gleamed black from head to toe.

'El Dorado!' Kirstie whispered.

The stallion had appeared out of nowhere. Undisputed leader of the wild herd, he ruled from a distance, always on the lookout for danger and ready to fight any upstart challenger.

He gazed calmly at Kirstie as if saying, *Remember me!*

This was the horse who was enveloped in rumour. Some said he was crazy, some that he had supernatural powers. But Kirstie knew that his reputation had been built out of sheer strength and intelligence, reflected from deep inside those dark eyes.

Sure, I remember you! I remember the ledge under Thunder Rock, the injuries you'd suffered, the help we were able to give.

People said that she, Rob and Lisa had saved El Dorado's life. But Kirstie knew that it was the stallion's own willpower and wisdom that had kept him alive. Nonetheless, it seemed to her that he was here now to return the favour.

She took a deep breath. 'Go ahead,' she murmured. 'Take me to Chiquitita!'

The horse dipped his magnificent head and moved off slowly. He led the way up the slope, in the shadow of the cave dwellings, and past them to a tricky climb over loose rocks and enormous granite boulders. They were gaining height, seeing glimpses of the Sierra Nevada in the far distance, rising above the line of aspens into territory where only scattered pine trees grew.

Once or twice, Kirstie had to pause to catch her breath, and El Dorado went on ahead. She glanced back at Great Bird Lake and up at a wasteland of bare rock, rising like grey whales, smooth and domed along the horizon. For a moment she doubted. Did the black mustang know what he was doing?

He turned to look at her, struck his hoof against the rock and urged her on.

She followed again, across the smooth, steep slope, towards a stand of crooked pines on the nearest ridge, glad of the breeze that blew here. But still she grew tired and the distance between her and the stallion lengthened. 'Go easy!' she pleaded, her legs aching, her lungs bursting.

El Dorado tossed his head and shook his mane. *You two-legged creatures sure are slow!*

Kirstie smiled grimly and pushed herself on. This mustang was doing her a major favour, but on his terms. 'Is Chiquitita hiding amongst the pines?' she asked, feeling that she couldn't go much further at El Dorado's speed.

He was making straight for the ridge, which was by now only a few hundred yards away. His hooves clattered noisily against the hard ground, warning of their approach.

Kirstie stared hard at the row of stunted trees. They seemed to grow twisted and leaning out of bare rock, with sparse branches and exposed roots which spread like thick tentacles above the surface. Some had been struck by lightning and all that remained were grey stumps or stripped trunks.

Now they were only a hundred yards short of the ridge and El Dorado was slowing down. He let Kirstie catch up with him and together they walked the final stretch.

He took her into the shadow of the trees on the windy ridge. The sun dappled the ground in a fluid pattern of light and shade. Patches of black and

patches of glaring white. Black and white. The colours of the missing paint.

Kirstie breathed in sharply. Was that real, or just a trick of the light? Could she really see Chiquitita standing patiently under the pine trees?

El Dorado stepped aside.

She saw the paint mare take a step towards them, into a circle of light.

The stallion turned his head towards Kirstie and made the familiar, head-dipping gesture. *Over to you!*

She nodded back. *Thank you!*

He backed away, tossed his head and wheeled around. The next second he was in full gallop, his powerful stride carrying him along the ridge. Her last sight was of him running free along the horizon, his mane and tail streaming in the wind.

Kirstie bit her lip. Chiquitita was looking to her now, understanding that the stallion had handed her over into the girl's care. The little mare came down from the ridge, straight up to Kirstie. There was no wildness left in her, only a desire to be taken back to the place where she was safe.

So Kirstie led her at first, down from the bare heights towards Great Bird Lake. Chiquitita stayed close by, content to be shown the way. Then, when they were back by the lake, with the cave dwellings towering above them and the glittering water stretching before them, Kirstie climbed on to the mustang's back. She would ride bareback by the water's edge to speed up their journey.

Chiquitita understood. She accepted Kirstie calmly and set off smoothly, only quickening her pace when she was sure that her rider was safe. Kirstie used her legs to guide the horse, knowing that, though she had no bit and bridle, pressure against her sides would do the trick.

They rode east across the hot plain with the sun behind them, a girl and a mustang travelling alone across the desert. Thorn bushes caught against Kirstie's legs and tumbleweed drifted across their path. The paintbrush cacti and Indian tobacco plants were vivid splashes of pink and yellow under the deep blue sky.

Kirstie sat easily on Chiquitita's broad back. She treasured each moment as they neared Squaw Lake – the mustang's graceful motion, the sense of being at one with the horse.

When she saw a Jeep appear in the distance, she was almost sorry. This was the end, then. Soon

Wayne would drive up and take charge. By sunset, Chiquitita would be safe in the barn and the dangers would be past. Everything as it should be.

But these moments would stay with her. She would never forget El Dorado's splendour and sweet Chiquitita's total trust.

'Are you nervous?' Lisa asked Kirstie.

'A little.'

'Me too.'

It was Friday morning and they were waiting for Wayne to drive Rob from the airport.

Lisa had brushed Chiquitita until her coat shone. Kirstie had braided her mane, Native American style. She was tacked up, Ms Sweet-and-Petite ready for Rob's return!

'You girls have prettied her up good!' Wayne had told them before he left. 'Watch she doesn't roll in the dirt!'

Time passed slowly. Kirstie gazed at the paint mare, remembering how Wayne had let her ride her all the way back to the ranch. He'd told her that Walter Gray was already en route to hospital in Reno and that the county sheriff was standing by ready to interview him at his bedside once the medics had set the broken bone in his leg.

'You girls did good,' he'd commented. 'I already spoke with Mary Ellen Black, and she's gonna press charges over the theft of her Cessna. She'd sure like to see Walter coolin' his heels in jail, and she's real sorry for not recognisin' the guy's faults.'

Kirstie had given a satisfied nod. 'Maybe you won't get such a hard time from Hope Valley from now on!'

Wayne had grinned. 'I wish!' he'd laughed.

By Thursday midday Wayne had cleared things with Jeff Oakley and been given the go-ahead to keep the paint mare. Kirstie and Lisa spent the rest of the day preparing her for Rob's return. They'd heard his grandpa had been taken off the critical list and it looked like he would make it. Now Rob said he was ready to come back to Squaw Lake.

'Don't tell him about Chiquitita!' Lisa had pleaded this Friday morning. She'd been throwing her stuff into a bag, ready to travel home to Colorado later that evening. 'Let him see how she is for himself!'

So now they were uptight, waiting for the big moment, looking back over an amazing vacation.

'I'll miss this place!' Kirstie murmured, gazing at Chiquitita. Her eyes filled up and she just managed to hold back the tears.

'You'll miss the wild horses,' Lisa put the record straight. 'El Dorado, Santa Ana, Chiquitita . . .'

'And all the two hundred others!' Kirstie admitted.

'That's a brave smile you're puttin' on, Kirstie Scott.' Lisa gave her arm a squeeze. 'But it's not foolin' anyone!'

They heard the Jeep come down the drive, saw Rob step out and straightaway come looking for his horse.

There she was in the yard. Her saddle gleamed; her eye was bright and welcoming.

Rob glanced at Kirstie and Lisa in total surprise. 'Like, wow!' he whistled.

They grinned at him. 'That's twenty dollars you owe me!' Kirstie said

'Can I ride her?' he asked her.

'Sure thing. She's your horse!' she replied.

Chiquitita stood good as gold as Rob slipped his foot in the stirrup. She didn't stir when he eased himself into the saddle.

Rob stroked her neck and rode her round the yard. 'Excellent!' he whispered.

He walked her out of the yard, down towards the lake, broke her into a trot, then into an easy lope.

It was a sight Kirstie had longed to see. She felt happy and sad, more happy, and then not sad at all. That was one neat horse and a kid who would love her for the rest of her life.

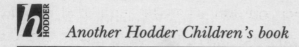
HORSES OF HALF-MOON RANCH 1:
Wild Horses

Jenny Oldfield

A wild and dangerous mountain setting and a daughter who lives, breathes and sleeps horses is a recipe for trouble for ranch owner, Sandy Scott. But Kirstie is undaunted by her mother's warnings. She's at her happiest riding the trails through the tall forests and deep canyons of the Meltwater Range . . .

Leading a trek in early summer, the fine weather turns. Creeks have flooded during torrential rain and now a landslide in a deep mountain gorge separates Kirstie and her pony, Lucky, from the rest of her group. They're trapped in Dead Man's Canyon with a herd of wild horses, one of whom has been hurt by falling rocks. Cold and alone in the gathering storm, how is Kirstie going to get help to the injured stallion?